CLAY

COLBY RODOWSKY

📚 HarperTrophy®
An Imprint of HarperCollins*Publishers*

Clay

Library of Congress Cataloging-in-Publication Data
Rodowsky, Colby F.
Clay / Colby Rodowsky.—1st Harper Trophy ed.
p. cm.
Summary: After their parents divorce, eleven-year-old Elsie and her
younger brother, Tommy, who is mentally "different," must deal with a
terrible secret that causes them and their mother to move from place to
place and stay in hiding.
ISBN 0-06-000618-8 (pbk.)
[1. Kidnapping, Parental—Fiction. 2. Brothers and sisters—Fiction.
3. Divorce—Fiction. 4. Autism—Fiction.] I. Title.
PZ7.R6185Cl 2004   2003020637
[Fic]—dc22

Typography by Amy Ryan
❖
First Harper Trophy edition, 2004
Visit us on the World Wide Web!
www.harperchildrens.com

For three cousins
with whom I share happy memories—
Edwina Koontz, Emily McDermott, and Bob Hearn

1

The truck was pulled up in front of the A
building, across the mingy plot of grass that separates it
from the B building, which is where I was. It was a
moving truck. Not one of those mile-long, shiny green
moving-van types with pictures of the world splashed
over it, but it was a truck, open and sort of square with
mattresses and chair legs sticking out the top. And the
people standing alongside of it were obviously moving
into the A building.

I wasn't all that interested in the beds and chairs and
lamps and even the monster-size TV that were piling up
on the sidewalk, though I have to admit they were a lot
better looking than the stuff in our already-furnished
apartment. *Already-furnished* means filled with a bunch
of left-behinds that various tenants through the years
hadn't bothered to take when they'd moved out of
Garden View.

It was the people *with* the truck I cared about now.

Cared about enough to unsmudge a corner of the window with my T-shirt and drag a wooden stool over with my foot. I settled down to watch.

"Hey, Tommy, there're people moving in across the way. Real people, with children. Come here and look."

He didn't, of course. Come to look I mean. I think that's mostly because my brother lacks what I heard somebody on *Oprah* once call "intellectual curiosity."

"Come *here*," I said again. "There's a girl looks like is my age and a boy about the same as you and a mother with spiky hair and a guy who's maybe the dad or maybe just the truck driver. I'm not sure which. Tell me what you think."

He didn't. I shot him a quick look, just long enough to see that he was swirling stones, before I went back to my window watching.

Tommy spends a lot of time swirling stones, or salt, or sugar, or sometimes just plain old dust, stirring whatever it is in circles, round and round. When we go outside, he collects tons of tiny stones and brings them in and stores them in a red Folgers coffee can. And when he doesn't know what else to do, he dumps them out on the table and swirls them with his fingers.

It drives Mom mad. My mother's name is Jude, and she works as a waitress at Nifties Fifties, which is a sort of diner, and mostly leaves me to take care of Tommy. Except when she drags us along and we get to sit in the far back booth by the kitchen door and eat french fries and ketchup and play the jukebox nonstop.

The Tommy-size boy across the way must have said something funny because all of a sudden the guy put down the chair he was carrying and pretend-swatted at him. Then he caught him in a giant bear hug and swung him around.

"He's the dad," I said to Tommy, but without looking at him. "On account of if he was just the truck driver, he wouldn't act so really interested." I watched as the father picked the chair up again and carried it inside. Tommy eventually came to stand beside me. (He's like that sometimes—doing what I asked once I've stopped asking.) We watched together as the girl and boy struggled with getting an empty bookcase inside, as the mother took an armload of boxes and then came back for another. As the dad lifted a mattress as if it were a feather and disappeared through the open door with it.

Tommy went back to swirling stones, but I kept standing there until all the belongings—the chairs and tables and boxes and bags and the monster TV—were taken inside. I stood there until the door to the A building was shut tight and the windows of one of the downstairs apartments were thrown open. I was still there, ages later, when the girl and the boy came back out, eating apples and carrying skateboards.

"Okay," I said. "That's it. Come on, we're going."

"Where?" said Tommy.

"Outside."

"Why?"

"To meet the new kids. Come *on*." Tommy didn't say anything, so I went on in my best I'll-explain-this-one-more-time voice. "There's a girl and a boy moved into the other building. I *told* you, and now they're out front, and if we go out kind of casual and make like we're going to the store for milk or something, then we can say 'hey' and they'll say 'hey' back to us, and we'll *know* them. Okay?"

Tommy didn't answer. He lined the gray stones down one side of the table and the white stones down the other.

"The boy might maybe let you play with his skateboard," I said to the top of my brother's head. "And you know what else, I'll bet he has a ton more stuff inside just waiting to be unpacked. I'll bet he has a soccer ball and a deck of Uno cards and maybe even a bike." I hadn't actually seen those things, but I said it anyway. "I'll bet he has an army truck and a dozen yo-yos and if we get to know them they'll ask us in someday to watch their big TV. And I'll bet the girl has a karaoke machine that I'm really gonna want to play with. Anyway, you *have* to come on account of Mom said I'm in charge and now I say so."

Tommy swooshed his stones, gray and white together

4

again, with one hand and swirled them around and around.

"If you come, I'll help you find more stones," I said in my sticky-nice voice. "We'll go to that driveway down by the corner where there are a bunch over to one side, and you can get maybe a hundred."

"Yeah?" said Tommy.

"Yeah. I'll get a plastic bag to carry them in." I grabbed a bag out of the kitchen cupboard and plucked a five-dollar bill from the table drawer for the milk and checked to make sure the string with the key on it was around my neck, all the while nudging Tommy toward the door. "Now remember, act cool," I said once we were outside. I steered him across the so-called grass to the front of the A building, where the girl and boy were sitting on the step.

"Hey," I said.

"Hey," the other girl said back, same as I knew she would.

"You new here?" I asked.

"New *here* and new to *Delaware*, too," she said. "I'm Manda Warner. Who are you?"

"My name is Elsie, and we live across the way, and we're on our way to the store and saw you sitting here."

"And I'm Checker. I'm seven and I'm her brother," the boy said, spinning the wheels of his upside-down skateboard.

"And that's *my* brother, and he's seven, too. His name is Tommy," I said.

"Can't he talk?" said Manda.

"Sure he can, when he's got something worth his while to say." I gave Tommy a sort of say-something poke, but he just stood there, folding and unfolding his plastic bag. "Which I guess he doesn't right now. I'm eleven. How about you?"

"I just turned eleven last week, and I got a karaoke machine for my birthday."

"I figured you did. I don't know how, but as soon as I saw you, I just figured you did. Can we play with it sometime?"

"Yeah, it's really awesome, but not today. My mom says toys are the last thing to be unpacked, and right now she's in there looking for sheets and all so she can make up the beds. Elsie what?"

"Elsie what what?" I said.

"Your name is Elsie what?" Manda said. "Like your *last* name."

"Oh," I said, and hesitated for a minute before going on. "McPhee." My mother's not all that keen on us talking to strangers—even kid strangers—and I was already getting a creepy feeling on the back of my neck.

"You all been here long? *Here*, at Garden View?"

"Awhile," I said.

"You go to that school around the corner? Maybe

we'll end up in the same class and Checker and Tommy in the same class, too. That'd be good, right?" said Manda.

"Not exactly," I said, rubbing at the back of my neck.

"What do you mean *not exactly*? How do you know you don't want to be in my class when you don't even know me?"

"I mean, I don't exactly go to that school," I said.

"How can you not exactly go someplace? Either you *go* or you *don't* go. Which is it?"

"I don't go," I said.

"How come you don't go?"

"Because my mother teaches us at home. And how come *you* ask so many questions?"

"'Cause I'm a Nosy Parker. That's what my grandmother used to call me. But if you think I'm bad, you should meet my mother. She'll find out your whole life story in two seconds flat, even all your deep dark secrets. Want to come inside and meet my mom and dad? I think there's some Kool-Aid we can make."

The creepy feeling up and down my neck was back, and I knew I didn't want to meet Manda's Super Nosy Parker mother. On the other hand, I thought maybe she would have been done making the beds by now and gone on to unpack the karaoke machine. "We could," I said. "Yeah."

Just then Tommy started tugging at my arm and

waving his yellow plastic bag in front of my face. "Except first I have to go with Tommy to get some stones."

"Stones?" said Manda. "What kind of stones?"

"Just stones. Little ones. He collects them, and there's a place down by the corner where there's a whole lot. But afterward we could come. Okay?"

I followed Tommy down the street while Manda followed me and Checker wove in and out between us on his skateboard. When we got to the driveway, Tommy squatted down, waddling like a duck from one side to the other as he gathered stones.

"Should I help him?" Manda asked.

"If you want," I said, getting down on the ground beside my brother. "He likes them really tiny, and gray or white. The purple-looking ones he puts back." For a while we picked and sorted without saying anything, and when the bag was full, I reached for it and tied a knot at the top. "Okay, Tommy, now it's time to go," I said, crossing my fingers and hoping he wasn't in one of his stubborn moods.

"Yeah," said Tommy as he stood up and trailed Checker along the sidewalk, and we all headed back to Garden View.

Manda's mother's hair was even spikier close up. It was yellow and sort of like wiry wool with cobwebs on the edges. "Oh, I *hate* to move," she said, putting down a box and holding out her hand first to me and then to Tommy. "But do you know that you're our first friends here in Delaware? Do you live in this building?"

"Across the way, Mom," Manda said.

"Well, good, good," Mrs. Warner went on, "because I promised Manda and Checker there'd be kids living nearby. It makes all the difference in the world—meeting someone right off. Are there other children in your family? Or is it just you and your mom and dad?"

Before I had to figure how to answer Mrs. Warner without really answering her, she was off to something else. "And how about school? What grade are you in? And do most of the children live right in the neighborhood? I hope I'll get to meet your mother soon."

"Mom, they don't go to school on account of their mother teaches them at home, and I've already told them you're a Nosy Parker, so now can we have some Kool-Aid?"

Mrs. Warner laughed and led the way into the kitchen, calling, "Come on, troops."

Tommy and I stayed until the sky was streaky gray and Manda's father left to pick up a pizza. He walked outside with us and called, as we started across the grass, "You all come back tomorrow, hear?"

Inside, our apartment was empty and filled with shadows. I turned on the lights and helped Tommy sort his stones. I talked him into taking a shower, and when he was done, I made grilled cheese sandwiches in the microwave and poured two glasses of milk and carried them into the living room, where we sat on the floor and watched *Jeopardy!* while we ate.

And afterward, last thing before he went to bed, I told my brother about a hundred times over, "Maybe we just won't say anything to Mom about the new kids who moved in today. You got that?"

That's the thing about Tommy. I'm never sure how much he really understands.

2

That night I sort of slept and sort of didn't sleep. Sort of real-dreamed and sort of daydreamed. Mostly about Manda and how we were going to be best friends.

The next day, starting with when my mother went to work, I had the kind of time I think *other* people have. At least for a while I did. But before, when Mom was still poking around the apartment, drinking coffee, and blow-drying her hair, I looked out the window and saw Manda on her front steps. That's when I crossed the fingers on both hands to keep her where she was and not let her come knocking on my door. It worked, and as soon as Mom had left and I was sure her car was all the way off the parking lot, I gathered up Tommy and his can of stones and my key and headed for Manda's. This time I didn't need to pretend we were on our way to the store. On account of we were friends.

"Hey," I said.

"Hey," she said. "What shall we do first? Karaoke?"

"Can we?" I asked.

"Yeah, sure. My mom worked so hard yesterday, she said today's her day to just chill out. C'mon in."

Manda's karaoke machine was even better than I imagined. First Mrs. Warner hooked a bunch of wires up to the TV, and when she had it all set and turned on, the words to the songs were right there on the screen while the music played. There was even a microphone for people to sing into. At first I thought I'd never be able to do it, but after Manda and Checker had each sung a solo and then a couple of duets, I bunched up all my courage and sang "America the Beautiful" the whole way through. After that the three of us sang "Yankee Doodle" together till almost at the end, when we started laughing so hard we couldn't get the words out and were rolling on the floor, holding our stomachs.

Except for Tommy, who sat the whole time with his back to us. Rocking.

When we finished laughing and were back on our feet, Manda's mom, who had come in to watch us, picked up the microphone and sang "Strangers in the Night," dancing around in front of the TV and sounding like a *real* singer.

"Now how about some lunch?" she said, turning off the machine. "I have hot dogs and rolls—okay?"

Much as I'd daydreamed of being friends with

Manda, I'd never actually thought about *eating* at her house. Because of Tommy, I mean. I was still standing there trying to decide what to say when Mrs. Warner touched me on the shoulder and said, "Why don't the four of you go on outside on the grass and I'll bring you a picnic? But tell me, Elsie, does Tommy like hot dogs?"

"Yeah, he does," I said. "But only the roll part."

"Is there something wrong with him?" asked Manda, looking down at Tommy, who still sat with his back to us.

"Nuh-uh," I said, shaking my head. "He's just different is all." This was the first time I'd ever said that, about my brother being different, and right away I started trying to figure what I'd say if she went on to ask *why* he was different, or *how*.

I didn't need to worry though, because Manda's mom gave her one of those don't-ask-that-kind-of-question looks, which must have been really hard what with her being a Nosy Parker and all. Instead she handed us a blanket to sit on and shooed us out the door, calling, "Three hot dogs and one empty roll coming up!"

After lunch Manda brought her Really Really Red nail polish outside, and we painted our toenails and fingernails. Then we lay on our backs on the grass, kicking our feet and waving our arms so our nails would dry, till Manda's mother called out the window saying, "You girls get up right this minute, that ground is still winter-cold."

Once we put our shoes and socks back on, we skate-boarded some, with me using Checker's board because he was busy making a convoy of his trucks. Then we all three sat in a row in front of Tommy and laid the trucks out between him and us, trying to get him to play. But Tommy seemed to scrunch further into himself, and eventually we went back to skateboarding.

"Want to have a snack?" said Manda as we were sitting on the steps thinking about what to do next. "I'll go in and get juice, and cookies if we have them."

"And I'll go home and make peanut-butter crackers," I said. "Besides, I have to take Tommy to the bathroom."

Back in our apartment Tommy settled himself on the floor in front of the television and sat staring at the blank screen until I turned the set on and found Barney for him. "Barney," he said. Then "Barney" again. The purple dinosaur skipped across the screen, and my brother started to rock.

I went into the kitchen and lined a bunch of crackers out on the counter and was just starting to spread peanut butter on them when I heard a key in the lock and my mother came in. "I thought you had to work both lunch *and* dinner today," I said.

"I do, but I ran home to change my shoes. I wore those new ones, and by the time the lunch crowd was finished, my feet were killing me. What's all this?" she said, pointing to the crackers.

"Just a snack. We were hungry, and I'm making us a snack."

"Well, put half of those back right away," Mom said. "You're not feeding an army, and besides, if you give Tommy all that, he won't eat any supper."

I reached for the crackers, and all of a sudden my mother's hand clamped down on my wrist, holding it flat against the counter, then picking it up and bringing my hand close to her face. "What's *this*?" she said, pointing to my Really Really Red nails.

"Fingernail polish," I said.

"Where did you get it?"

"I found it," I said, not even taking time to think.

"You found it where?"

"Outside. On the sidewalk in front of our apartment. I took Tommy out for a little walk, and it was just lying there, next to the grass."

"You mean to tell me you used somebody's old nail polish that you just *found* someplace? Don't you know it could have been diseased, or poisoned? Don't you?"

"I guess, but I didn't think—"

"Where is it now?" my mother asked. "Let me see it."

"In the Dumpster. I threw it in the Dumpster. I mean, once I did my fingers and toes, there wasn't any more and I just threw it away."

"Don't you *ever* do anything like that again. Do you hear me, Elsie?"

I nodded, half afraid that if I said anything, my voice would shake. I felt crawly all over for lying to my mother like that, but I knew for sure that there was no way I could have told her about Manda and Checker and the hot-dog picnic.

Mom changed her shoes. She kissed Tommy hello and good-bye and stopped in the kitchen to talk to me. "Remember what I told you," she said, her eyes burning right into me. "And don't take Tommy outside anymore today, it's turning cool. Got it?"

"Got it," I said, as she closed the door behind her.

I watched at the window to make sure she was really gone, and as soon as I saw Manda come out of her building, I grabbed my key and dashed over to meet her. "I can't play anymore today on account of my mom came home to change her shoes and she said it's turning cool and she doesn't want Tommy outside and I've got to get back because he doesn't even know I'm gone. But I'll see you tomorrow. Okay?"

"Yeah, sure, okay," said Manda, putting her juice pitcher and cups down on the steps. "But hey—tell me your phone number, and I'll call you later."

I turned away from her and started across the grass plot, not wanting to have to stand there and face her while I said, "I can't. We don't have a phone."

Tommy and I spent a boring rest-of-the-day watching boring television until it was time for him to go to

16

bed. After that I got out the Egypt book from the library and read about mummies and looked at the pictures, even one of a mummy cat.

I woke the next morning just after dawn, but it was gray and yucky out and I scrunched down lower in the bed and fell into a deep sleep. When the sound of the voice finally reached me, it sounded as if it were coming from far away. Like down at the bottom of a well, maybe.

"EL-SIE EL-SIE EL-SIE EL-SIE"

I batted at it and tried to push it away.

"EL-SIE EL-SIE EL-SIE EL-SIE"

The voice went on, snaking in from outside and wrapping around me, nudging me awake.

"EL-SIE EL-SIE"

It's Manda, and she's on the other side of the window calling me, I thought, as I shot up out of bed and reached to flip the shade.

But just then I heard Mom come out of her bedroom, and I flew back under the sheets. "What the devil kind of noise is that?" my mother shouted as she made her way across the living room, rattling the chain on the front door and yanking it open. I heard her go through the vestibule to the door of the building. And I heard her outside.

"Just what do you think you're doing?" my mother yelled. "Get away from that window. Don't you know it's practically the middle of the night and there're some of us who're trying to sleep? Don't you? And what are you doing here anyway? You answer me right this minute."

There was a pause that I guess was Manda saying something, though I couldn't hear her, and then my mother started in again. "There isn't any Elsie in there who's coming out to play with you, so you just get yourself back where you belong, or I'll speak to the management. And don't let me see you around here again. You got that? You got it?"

My face burned, and I ground it into the pillow. A part of me wanted to race over and bang on the window for Manda to come back. A part of me didn't dare. And then Mom was there, pushing the door to my room open and standing over me, hissing and whispering both at the same time. To keep from waking Tommy, I guess.

"Do *you* know anything about that? Do *you* know who that girl was?"

I groaned and pretended to stir in my sleep.

"Have you been out there talking to people when I've told you a hundred times over not to do that? Told you and Tommy to stay to *yourselves*."

I groaned again and stretched out my legs and breathed deep, sleeping breaths.

"Oh, never mind—I'm going back to bed, and we'll settle this later," my mother said as she headed into her room, shutting the door behind her.

After she left, the room was quiet, except for the snorty-snuffly noises Tommy makes when he sleeps. Then I began to hear the echo of Manda's voice. *"El-sie, El-sie, El-sie."* I rolled over and saw the words splashed across my ceiling in one of those balloon things, like in cartoons. *"El-sie, El-sie, El-sie."*

The balloon broke apart and dissolved and reformed again, only this time it said *"L.C., L.C., L.C."* The bed beneath me shook, and I held on to the sides. *"L.C., L.C., L.C."* I whispered the words "Linda Clay," and all of a sudden a door inside of me creaked open.

I crept out of bed and went over to the table, grabbing for a paper and pencil and staring at them for a minute before I started to write. *"Elsie McPhee—L.C. McGee—Linda Clay McGee—Linda Clay."* I scribbled the words over and over, down the middle of the page and up the edges. I turned the paper over and kept going. *"Tommy McPhee—Timmy McGee—Timmy Timmy Timmy."*

The door in my head creaked open wider, and I clutched hold of the paper and hurried back to bed. Memories came flooding in, and I closed my eyes and stuffed my fingers in my ears, pushing them away, keeping them out. But I knew, sure as anything, that now that the door was open, they'd be there waiting for me.

When Tommy woke up, we went into the kitchen

and I fixed him Cheerios and a glass of juice. Afterward, when he was done, I washed the dishes and turned on the TV so he could watch *Sesame Street*, which is actually too young for him except he still likes it. Especially Oscar the Grouch. Meanwhile, I tried not to think.

I don't know how long we'd been sitting there like that—Tommy watching and me not thinking—before Mom came out of her room. "Ye-gads, what a night," she said as she struggled into her robe. "I was late getting home from work, and then I couldn't get to sleep, and when I finally did, that kid turned up outside, screaming like a banshee. Did you hear all that racket?"

"Nuh-uh," I said, shaking my head and staring at the TV.

Mom reached for the jar of instant coffee and then came over to where I was sitting, leaning close and squinting her eyes at me. "You're sure you don't know anything about that, Miss Elsie McPhee? Girl about your age yelling to beat the band? Wouldn't be somebody you've taken up with, would it? Not somebody you've been maybe hanging out with when I've told you a hundred times over just to watch your brother and stay to yourself? How about that?"

I crossed my fingers until they hurt and said, "It's nobody I know."

"Sounded to me like she was saying 'Elsie' if she was saying anything," my mother said.

I shook my head again.

"How about you, Tommy-kins? You know anything about that?" my mother asked, turning to my brother.

I held my breath and willed him not to speak. He licked his lips and didn't say anything, and then aeons later picked up his Folgers coffee can and held it close as he rocked back and forth. Back and forth.

All of a sudden I wanted to uncross my fingers and tell my mother the truth. Wanted to tell her about Manda and her family and how they'd just moved in and about the karaoke machine and the hot-dog picnic and what it was like to do *real* things that *real* people do. But something about the way Mom looked, all pinched and sort of wild, made me bite down hard on the words and swallow them back.

When my mom was done with her toast and coffee, I went and got my books and spread them out on the table. Which is what I do a lot of mornings. But instead of going on with the story about the ancient Egyptians and pharaohs and pyramids and all, my mother jiggled her foot against the table leg and stared at the wall just over my head. "I can't deal with this today," she said, pushing the books away and getting up. "I have things on my mind. You just go on by yourself."

"But I've already read this, and even written stuff down like you said I should." I pushed my notebook to the edge of the table.

"Read your library book then," my mother said, dropping her plate and mug in the sink.

"I've read that, too. Can we go today and get some more?" I asked.

"Just stop bugging me, Elsie. I told you I've got things on my mind. Help Tommy with his letters if you're looking for something to do. I think he's really catching on, don't you?"

"Yeah, Mom. Sure," I said, not looking at her, on account of we both knew that was a lie.

Since Mom only had to work the dinner shift, it was the middle of the afternoon when she was ready to leave for work. "I'm just going in for a while to pick up my pay," she said, leaning on the kitchen counter. "And while I'm gone, don't you dare think about leaving this apartment. And don't you dare open this door—not even for the president of the United States. Not even for the pope. You understand that?"

"I understand," I said, staring down at the crack in the kitchen floor.

Once she was gone, I got out the plastic bowling set that Tommy sometimes does and sometimes doesn't play with, and set it up. This was a *doesn't* day. I rolled the ball into the pins a bunch of times, trying to give him the idea. He watched me for a spell and then took up his coffee can and dumped the stones onto the table and started to swirl them.

I kicked the pins out of the way and went over to the window, pulling the curtains aside with my fingers and looking out. I stayed there maybe forever, and just when I was about to give up, the front door of the A building opened and Manda and Checker and their mother and father came out. They started down the walk, and then Manda stopped and turned and stared straight at my window, as if she was waiting for me or something. I let go of the curtain and jumped back, flattening myself against the wall and gasping to catch my breath. And when I looked again, she was gone.

I kicked the bowling ball as hard as I could and sent it flying into the corner. "Come on, Tommy," I said. "You want tuna fish or grilled cheese tonight?"

3

My mother came home just when I was about
to get Tommy ready for bed. It had been another one of
those stretched-out, boring nights, the kind when I
wished we at least had cable, or a VCR, or extra library
books. When I wished, more than anything, that I had
someone to talk to, other than my brother. I mean
Tommy's great and all, but he is what I heard someone
on TV once call "conversationally challenged." And
another thing, Tommy doesn't seem to know the difference between *bored* and *not bored*. As long as he has his
stones.

"I got my check and I've been to the bank, and now
we're out of here," Mom said, throwing her purse on the
counter and kicking off her shoes. She had that same
pinched and sort of wild look she'd had earlier, only
more so.

I watched and waited, not saying anything as she
dragged empty cardboard cartons out of the closet by

the front door. "That big old yellow suitcase is in the back of your cupboard," she said. "You go ahead and get that out and pack up your and Tommy's stuff."

"But Mom—" I said.

"Don't you 'But Mom' me."

"But Mom," I went on anyway, "where are we going?"

"Out of here. I told you we're out of here." She was already pulling boxes of cereal and cans of spaghetti sauce off the cabinet shelves and shoving them into a carton.

"But why are we leaving at night? Why not tomorrow or next week or—"

"Because I need to feel safe, and I don't feel safe here anymore."

"Safe from what?" I asked.

"Never you mind safe from what. You just do as you're told. And don't forget to get Tommy's slippers out from under the bed," my mother said.

I looked over at my brother. He was just sitting there with his arms locked across his chest. Rocking.

There wasn't much to pack. We just had our clothes and Tommy's bowling set and a couple of games and the hair dryer and Band-Aids and stuff from the bathroom. Even the sheets and the tattery towels were part of the "already furnished" deal, and Mom just folded them and left them on top of the kitchen table, along with the keys to the apartment and our library books. "I hope somebody will see to these," she said as she struggled out the door with the yellow suitcase and nodded for me to follow with one of the boxes. When the car was loaded, we went back inside to go to the bathroom. "We'll drive till I'm tired," said Mom as she checked the kitchen cupboards one last time. "But right now I'm feeling pretty wired, so that could be all night."

"Come on, Tommy." Mom held out her hand to him, but Tommy sank down lower in his seat and wrapped his feet around the chair legs, holding tight. My mother reached for his shoulder, but he fell forward, like some floppy kind of rag doll.

"Bring your brother, Elsie," said Mom, sighing and heading for the door. "Just bring him."

Part of me wanted to sit down next to him and refuse to leave, and for a minute I wondered what would happen if I did. But instead I knelt on the floor in front of him, propping him up so he had to look at me. "Come on, Tommy. It's time to go. And you know what? There're going to be tons more stones where we're going, all just waiting for you."

"Where?" said Tommy.

"Somewhere," I said. "Now come on. *Please.* It's just for a spell, and then we'll be right back here." The last twelve words were a lie, but sometimes I say anything I have to, to keep Tommy from getting all riled up.

I got Tommy settled on the backseat and fastened his seat belt, and then I climbed in next to him.

"What's that make me—the chauffeur?" asked Mom, patting the seat beside her and turning to look at me.

"Yep," I said. Only quick, before she could say I was sassing her, I added, "It's on account of Tommy and wanting to make sure he doesn't freak out when he sees we're really *moving*." The truth was, I didn't want to sit next to my mother. Didn't want to see her pointy chin jutting out as she drove or hear the *thrum thrum thrum* of her fingers on the steering wheel. I didn't want to be in this car on this road, going wherever we were going.

I looked over at Tommy, but he had zonked out almost as soon as the car started. All of a sudden I wanted to punch him and scream at him and ask him why he was asleep instead of awake and caring about what was happening to us. That's the thing about Tommy—you can never be sure when he's going to *care* about things.

My head felt ready to explode, and I twisted my seat belt and pushed my feet hard against the seat in front of me. Much as I hated Garden View, I wanted to be back there. Or at the place before that, or the place before *that*. Garden View, or Valley Green, or Mountain Glen, or wherever. No matter how they sounded, they were all cheesy with the same skimpy towels and lumpy beds and flickering TVs—and there were never *gardens* or *valleys* or *mountains* anyplace in sight.

I started to shiver all over and wrapped my arms across my chest as I said, "Okay, where are we going *this* time?"

"Don't you be giving me a lot of mouth for trying to keep us safe," my mother snapped. "If I've told you once, I've told you a hundred times, there's evil out there just waiting to grab you and Tommy up."

Like you grabbed us up. The words pulsed inside my head, but before I got the nerve to say them out loud, she went on. "Anyway, this is all your fault—for talking to that girl. And don't tell me you didn't. Don't tell me any more lies about finding that nail polish outside. *She* gave it to you—didn't she. And now *you're* the reason we have to move. You never heard me say not to go mixing with strangers? You never heard me say as how we don't need people snooping in our lives? Just answer me that."

"Yeah, I guess," I said. I let out a sigh and then took in a deep breath before I said, "Well, at least can we go to real school *this* time? And maybe get a phone?"

"Right, sure," my mother said. "Get a phone so anybody can be calling us up, trying to sell us things, snooping on us? Is that what you want? And you think I'm really going to turn you loose with a bunch of people we don't know from Adam? You think I'm really going to do that? Besides, I teach you everything you need to know, and you're a smart girl. You don't need school."

"Tommy does," I said. "Tommy's seven years old and he's never been to school and he needs to go and maybe he wouldn't be the way he is if he *did* go."

I saw my mother's shoulders tense up and felt the car swerve as she yanked on the steering wheel, pulling it first one way and then the other. "What do you mean 'the way he is'?"

I was pretty sure it was a question that wasn't meant to be answered, but I answered it anyway. "You know, how he doesn't even know his letters and scribble-scrabbles when he goes to draw and doesn't hardly *say* anything or *care* about anything except for stones and won't look anybody straight in the eye."

The car swerved again as Mom said, "There's nothing wrong with Tommy—just because he keeps things to himself and doesn't blab all over the place like some people I know. There's nothing wrong with your brother. You got that, Elsie? Elsie? Elsie?"

Elsie Elsie Elsie—I heard Manda calling to me the way she had early in the morning. I heard *L.C. L.C. L.C.* I heard *Linda Clay*. And then the door that had creaked a little bit open that morning flew all the way open, and the memories I'd been trying not to remember rushed in.

It was just after the divorce, and we were living with our father on account of the judge said that's where we should live. He was big and round with fuzzy gray hair (the judge, not my father), and when I had to go in and sit in a chair alongside of his desk, he called me Linda Clay instead of L.C., which is what most people called me, and asked me if I knew why my parents were getting a divorce.

"Because they fight," I remembered saying.

"Well, yes," the judge said, rolling a pen back and forth across his desk. "Sometimes mothers and fathers fight, and when they can't figure a way to stop fighting, then sometimes they decide to live apart and get a divorce. And sometimes it's very hard for the children to understand what the fighting is all about."

"Except I know," I said. "They fight about everything. They fight about my dad being a lawyer and my mom breaking all the laws, like driving too fast and not wearing seat belts and walking on the grass when the sign says not to. They fight about how, when my dad takes me and Timmy to do stuff on Saturdays, we go to places like the courthouse or on a walking tour of downtown, and my mom says that's boring, boring, boring, and what's he want to do—turn me into Judge Poker-face." I stopped and looked at him to see if maybe I shouldn't have said that about Judge Poker-face in front of a real-life judge, but he didn't seem to care. "And they fight about my mom being an artist," I went on, "and how every time she goes back to art school, she quits again because she never wants to listen to what the teachers have to say."

And mostly they fight about Timmy, I thought to myself but didn't say out loud, because even though I was only seven at the time, I was pretty sure I shouldn't tell that to the fuzzy-haired judge or anyone else. But they did. They fought about how my dad said they should take Timmy to a special doctor because of the way he acted or didn't act and the way he'd never really look at you no matter what and the way if somebody picked him up he'd get all stiff or else just fold over like some old quilt and never cuddle like little kids pretty much do. And all the while my mom said that there was nothing wrong with Timmy, that he was just thoughtful and deliberate and why should he act like other kids when he was perfect and they weren't.

And the biggest fight of all was after my father made an appointment with the special doctor and then something really important came up at work and he couldn't go, so my mom said she'd take Timmy by herself. Then that night she said that she had been right all along and that the doctor said there was nothing wrong with Timmy and that he *was* perfect. The only trouble with that was, she never really took him for the appointment and made up all the things the doctor was supposed to have said.

It was after that that my mother and father got the divorce and I had to go in and talk to the judge and Mom moved out and got her own apartment and it was arranged that she would sometimes come to get Timmy and me and take us places. My brother and I were to stay at our regular house with our regular father (who never fought with anybody anymore) and with Nana and Popoo (his parents and our grandparents), who lived nearby, coming in to help a lot. And for when they couldn't come, there was Blanche the baby-sitter, who was there the day it happened.

I dragged myself back to the present, blinking at the inside of the car, at Tommy, who was asleep and slumped against the seat belt with little bits of slobber in the corners of his mouth. I watched the back of my mother's head and heard the low, jangly sound of jazz from the car radio. Everything was dark except for the red glow of taillights of the cars in front of us and the green exit signs as we swooshed past them. But no matter how hard I tried to keep them away, the old memories crept back around me. Memories of that last day with Blanche the baby-sitter.

It had been a school holiday—not something big like Presidents' Day or spring break, but just a holiday—and the day before my father was to take Timmy to the special doctor. He had made a second appointment, and this time he was really going to go himself. In the morning I'd hung around the house, playing Barbies and watching my brother as he rocked in front of the TV. My best friend, who was named Margaret and lived next door, and Lily, my second-best friend from across the street, were both gone for the day, and I was bored. After lunch, I talked Blanche into taking us to the playground, which was sort of babyish but still better than sitting in the house all afternoon.

When we got to the playground, Blanche sat on one of the swings with Timmy on her lap, not really swinging but shuffling back and forth. I headed for the farthest-away swing in the row, pushing myself back and then pumping as hard as I could, pumping, pumping, pumping, until I was sailing. Up and back. Up and back. It was when I was way up one time, higher than the tree branches, that I saw my mother getting out of her car and coming toward us.

"Hi, everybody," she said when I had let the swing slow a little and jumped off, landing at her feet. "I checked the house, and when no one was home, I thought I'd try here." She turned to Blanche and said, "It's such a glorious day, I'm going to take L.C. and Timmy for ice cream."

"Well, I don't know," I remember Blanche saying. "I

mean, Mr. McGee didn't say anything about that."

Mom shook her head, her bushy black hair going every which way, and said, "What's to say? You've known me for years, Blanche. I'm their mother, and we're going for a little ice cream. Now you run along back to the house and put your feet up for a bit, and we'll be there before you know it. Come on, kids."

And somehow, like maybe she had waved a magic wand, Timmy and I were in my mother's car on our way to Baskin-Robbins.

At the ice cream store, we got our cones and sat on a bench outside eating them. I had mint chocolate chip and Timmy had vanilla with sprinkles, only his mostly dripped down the front of him. Then, without even wiping Timmy's hands and face, Mom hurried us back into the car, and when we pulled away from the store, she turned left instead of right.

We had been going a whole five minutes by the clock before I got up the nerve to say, "This isn't the way home."

"You're not going home, L.C.," my mother said, without even turning around. "You're not going home ever again."

4

My mother swung the car into a rest stop and
turned to look at Tommy and me. I put on my best sleep
act, and after a minute I heard her get out and lock the
door. Once she was gone, I opened my eyes carefully but
didn't really move because all of a sudden I had this
weird feeling that I was sitting in a bubble bath of memories—and if I did move, the bubble-memories would
pop and disappear. And I'd never catch them again.

Before I had a chance to slip into that other time,
though, Mom was back. The smell of her coffee filled
the car as she started the engine, clicked on the radio,
and pulled out onto the highway. I stared at the back of
her head, at the way her mop of dark hair seemed to
grow and grow and fill half of the space in the front seat.

It had been the same way that other time, too, except
that it had been daylight, at least when we started out,
and Timmy and I had been sticky with ice cream.

"What do you mean we're not going home ever

again," I had said, jamming my feet down as if I could stop the car. "What do you *mean*? We've got to see Daddy, and Nana, and Popoo. What about Blanche? We've got to see Blanche on account of you told her we'd be right back. And besides, Timmy has his appointment tomorrow."

"Your father doesn't want you anymore," my mother said. For a minute I couldn't get my breath, and I turned to look at Timmy, to see if he had heard what I thought I heard. My brother was licking ice cream off his fingers, one at a time.

"What did you say?" I waited till she stopped for a light and then climbed into the front seat.

"You heard me. Your dad doesn't want you anymore. You *or* Timmy. And that's all nonsense about taking Timmy to a specialist. There's nothing wrong with your brother. So figure I'm doing your father a favor, taking you kids off his hands like this. Figure now he can get out of that house and get himself an apartment. Probably even move to another city."

"No, he never would!" I screamed. "Daddy loves us and he loves our house and that's where he wants to live forever. And besides, there's Tiger—that's where *he* lives, and cats *hate* to move, and Daddy knows that." I was sure that I was choking and hunched my shoulders, sucking the air in and pushing it out. I thought about my father sitting in the hammock in the backyard and showing me the Big Dipper. I thought about him stringing lights on the Christmas tree and the worried look he always got when he hugged Timmy good night. "Daddy's going to miss us," I said. "What if he thinks we got lost or something? What if he's waiting for us? What if—"

"What if, what if, what if. What if he is?" Mom said, speeding through a red light while horns honked all around us. "Maybe it'd just serve him right for talking trash to that judge and convincing him my children would be better off with their father. That *he* was more stable and would take better care of *my* kids. That *he* would get help for my son, who doesn't need any help at all. Right, Timmy-o? Right?"

Timmy didn't say anything.

My mother's face was spotted all over with meanness, and I pulled back against the car door. When I got the nerve, I said, "What about Nana and Popoo? What about when they call and want Timmy and me to come over? Or when they want me to dog-sit for Sandy, or Nana makes oatmeal cookies? Or when Popoo needs help with his crossword puzzle and I'm not there to tell it to him?" I thought about the game my grandfather and I played, where he asked me for answers to his puzzles and then, when he thought of them on his own, always pretended I had given them to him. "What about that, huh?"

"What about it?" my mother said. "Your grandparents

don't want to be bothered now that they're retired. They want to travel, go places, do things. That's what people their age do, so I'm doing *them* a favor, too."

"I don't believe you," I said, slapping at the dashboard. "You're making it up, and I'm going to run away and call them so's they can come get me and Timmy."

"I wouldn't try it, little miss. I'm all you have now, and don't you forget it. Father gone, grandparents gone. Why, you just go ahead and call, and you'll hear *'This number has been disconnected.'*" My mother said the last part in a tinny robot voice, then she went on. "Squeal on me, and you'll be in big trouble. Do you understand what I'm saying to you, Linda Clay? I'm *all* you have."

The same quivery feeling I had felt that day came back to me now, and I fought my way up out of the memories. I stretched my arms and legs and twisted my neck, peering at the clock. "We've been driving forever and I'm tired and besides I've got to pee, so when are we going to get somewhere?" I asked.

"Pretty soon. We're coming into Richmond now, and we'll stop here," my mother said. She turned off the highway and drove through deserted streets, past closed-up gas stations and darkened stores. "There ought to be a place to stay somewhere around here."

After a few more blocks, she pulled in under a blinking puke-green sign that said M O T L. "You kids wait here while I go in and register," my mother said, getting

38

out and slamming the car door, jerking Tommy awake so that he started right in to moan. He does that sometimes, especially when things change from the way he wants them to be. I put my hand on his arm and felt him stiffen. "It's okay, Tommy. You've had a nap and now you're awake, and we're going to spend the night at a motel. It's okay."

Tommy moaned louder and started to rock, pushing against his seat belt and then falling back.

When Mom came out, she dropped the room key on top of the dashboard, saying, "Number seventeen. The creep in there said it was around back."

"Tommy's awake," I said.

"Yeah, I hear him. Hi, Tommy, have a good sleep?" she said, turning around and reaching to touch him. My brother didn't look at her but kept on moaning and rocking.

"Keep him quiet, will you, Elsie?" she said as she started the car and headed around the side of the motel. "The creep acted like he never heard of anybody checking in at three in the morning. What do they do—roll the sidewalks up at ten o'clock around here?"

The bedspreads and carpet in room 17 were the same green as the sign outside, except that there were spots on the carpets and raveled threads hanging off the spreads. Mom steered Tommy into the bathroom, but when he came out, instead of getting into bed, he squatted on the floor, rocking and starting to howl a funny animal kind of howl.

There was a sudden thumping on the wall, and an angry voice called out, "Don't you people know it's the middle of the night? What are you *doing* in there?" There was another thump, and I held my breath, afraid that some hairy fist might break through and reach out and clobber us all.

Tommy didn't even look up.

"It's okay, Tommy," I said, getting down on the floor beside him. "It's okay. This is Virginia, and you're going to like it here. This is Virginia, and there're lots of cool things to do here. There're trees and flowers and history stuff. We'll find a library and I'll take you there and we'll get books and I'll read them to you, same as we've always done. We'll read Jessie Bear and the mouse-cookie book and we'll watch *Sesame Street* on the TV and find Oscar and Bert and Ernie, we'll find Big Bird." I babbled on, making my voice go flat, saying the same things over and over. "It's okay. This is Virginia, and you're going to like it here. And we'll find stones. I promise you that tomorrow we'll find stones. Stones, stones, stones."

Tommy went from a howl to a moan. His voice grew softer, his eyes closed, and he finally slumped over in a heap. My mother dragged a spread off one of the beds and bunched it around him. I slid a pillow under his head.

"I'm so tired, I'm senseless," my mother said, crawling into bed. "And tomorrow—today—I have to find us a nice apartment, or maybe even a house." She reached over and turned off the light.

I stretched out on the other bed, looking up at the dot of light from the smoke detector and listening to my mother and brother breathe. After a while I got up and made my way over to a chair by the window, pulling back the curtain so I could see out to the parking lot. It won't be a house, I thought. It'll be another crummy apartment like we always end up in. Like the one we ended up in the day my mother stole us from our father.

That first apartment had been in a complex called Mountain Glen in a town somewhere in New Jersey. As soon as we walked in the door, I knew that Mom had already been there. Her sketch pads and pastels and pencils were piled up on the counter; there was food in the kitchen cupboards and a jar of instant coffee on the stove. And a collection of games was spread out over the wobbly table in the living room. I guess they were supposed to make us think we were on some kind of vacation, except that Timmy couldn't play games, even the easy baby ones, and I knew sure as anything that this wasn't a vacation.

"Nice, huh?" my mother said, stepping back and throwing out her arms in a ta-dum sort of way. "And because this is a special day, we'll even go out for pizza—extra cheese, pepperoni, whatever you kids want—and before you know it, you'll feel right at home."

"I'm not hungry," I said. "And I *won't* feel at home."

"You will," said Mom, "because as I pointed out to you in the car, this is the only home you have now, and I'm your only parent."

I looked over at the door, trying to figure if I could grab my brother and run, but when I turned to Timmy, he was crouched down in the space between a chair and the wall, rocking. I knew I couldn't move him fast enough. I knew I couldn't go without him. And I was pretty sure my mother knew that, too, because she went into her bedroom and left us alone. When she came out, she had changed her shirt and put on lipstick. She had her purse under her arm.

"Come on, let's go get that pizza, and we can eat it there or bring it home. Either way. You decide."

The pizza place was noisy and crowded, and as soon as we got inside the door, Timmy started turning in circles and flapping his hands. "We'd better get carryout," I said. "It'd be easier, with him and all."

"Oh, that's nonsense," said Mom. "Timmy'll be all right, won't you, baby? Besides, it's important for him to learn to eat in restaurants." She reached out to rumple his hair, but he kept right on turning, as if he didn't see her.

"You said it was up to me. You said for me to decide, and I say we'd better get carryout."

"Fine, fine, whatever you say, L.C. Now, does pepperoni suit you?" said Mom as she headed for the counter, not even waiting for an answer.

"I'm not going to eat it anyway," I whispered, though I wasn't too sure about that anymore because the pizza smells were making my stomach growl, and I was getting hungrier every second.

"Fifteen minutes," said Mom. "We're number fourteen, so listen for that."

We stood back against a wall, except for Timmy, who stayed where he was, with everybody having to step around him. I watched the pizza man twirling the dough, and the people in the restaurant part eating their dinners. I looked at the posters of tons of different kinds of pizza—pepperoni, double cheese, green peppers, and even pineapple, and right there, between the green peppers and the pineapple, was a phone hanging on the wall.

"We could call Daddy," I said, tugging on my mother's arm. "We could call, and then he'd know where we were and he wouldn't worry."

"I told you he won't be worrying. I told you he'll be busy with other things."

"We could call anyway on account of I know he'd want us to. I just *know* it."

"You really want to call? Is that what you want?" Mom asked, pushing her way through the line to get to the phone. She put some money in the slot and punched a bunch of numbers and then held the receiver up to her ear. "See? What did I tell you—nobody's home. He's off somewhere already," my mother said as she handed me the phone.

I listened to the ringing for a very long time before I gave it back to her. "I bet he's out looking for us. That's where he is. And he'll be back soon," I said, as I tried to swallow the tears I could feel starting up.

"Do you think your father went out without leaving the answering machine on if he really wanted a call? Without leaving someone there to answer the phone? Do you?"

And before I could think of what to say next, the pizza man called number fourteen, and my mother hung up the phone and headed for the counter. "Come on," she said after she paid. "Let's go home."

Back at the apartment, Mom served the pizza. She poured lemonade into glasses and put them on the table. "And now I have a surprise," she said as she led Timmy over and settled him into his place. "From now on I'm going to teach you at home." She held a chair out for me, then sat across from the two of us, all the while reciting " 'No more lessons, no more books, no more teacher's dirty looks' " in a singsongy voice. "Except there *will* be lessons and books, but they'll be right here, where it's safe."

"But Mom, I'm almost done with first grade, and next year I might maybe get Mr. Benson—and he's the greatest."

"You only think that because you haven't seen me in action," my mother said. "We'll have drawing and reading, math and, oh, everything."

"But what about Timmy? He needs to go to preschool—Daddy said so—where they'll try to help him and get him to be like other kids."

"Your father's wrong." My mother sort of spat the words. "There's nothing the matter with my son, and I've been telling him that for years. Isn't that so, Timmy?" She reached out and ran her fingers through his dark, sticking-up hair. "And besides, if Timmy needs preschool, we'll *do* preschool. You and I together. Right here."

When we were done picking at our pizza, Mom cleared the table and brought a pad of white paper and colored markers and put them in front of me. "First lesson," she said, sitting down next to me.

"Not tonight. I'm tired," I said. "And besides, nobody goes to school at night."

"We do," she said, "because rule number one is, you can't go to school until you know your name. Right?"

"But Mom, I *know* my name. I've known it forever,

and even Timmy knows *his* name. What are you talking about?"

"Your new names. That's part of the fun." She grabbed a green marker and wrote ELSIE McPHEE and TOMMY McPHEE in big letters. "There you go. Names that are close, but different enough to keep you safe. And I'm Jude instead of Julie. Now you write them." She handed me a red marker.

I drew an X through both names.

She wrote them again, only larger this time. "Don't trifle with me, Elsie," my mother said. "From now on Linda Clay is gone, L.C. is gone, Timmy is gone. The McGees are gone. Do you get that?" Her face was squinty-eyed and scary when she spoke. Then she caught hold of me and hugged me till my ribs hurt.

I shivered and pulled myself back to the present. I stared out at the parking lot, watching a cat jump from the hood of a car onto a Dumpster. When I got tired of watching the cat, I tiptoed across the room, stepping over Tommy, and crawled into bed. I grabbed a handful of bunched-up sheet and made my mind go blank.

5

When I woke up the next morning, Tommy was sitting on the floor in front of the turned-off television, and my mother was nowhere in sight. A note, propped on the table, said, *Hi Elsie, I've gone to find us a place to live. Back soon. Here's breakfast for you and Tommy. Mom.* A lightning-bolt arrow pointed to a carton of juice and a box of doughnuts.

Turning on the TV, I flipped through the channels until I found *Sesame Street*. The picture jittered and the voices wobbled, but my brother didn't seem to care. He stared at a spot on the wall, behind the set. "Come on, Tommy. Mom left breakfast," I said.

He didn't answer, or move, either.

I got a couple of plastic cups out of the bathroom for the juice and tore the top off the box to make a plate, putting a doughnut on it and plunking it all down on the floor in front of him. I mean, the way I figured it, the carpet couldn't get any grosser. No matter what Tommy did.

After I ate, I was heading for the bathroom, set to brush the yucky powdered-sugar taste off my teeth, when I remembered that the yellow suitcase stuffed with Tommy's and my clothes was still in the trunk of Mom's car. With our toothbrushes inside. I settled for scrubbing at my teeth with the corner of a towel, then took a shower and put my dirty clothes back on.

Tommy was still sitting where I'd left him, still staring at the wall, but the juice and half a doughnut were gone. "Want to do something?" I asked. "Want to go outside?"

He didn't answer.

I sat on the end of one bed, then on the other. I jerked the curtains open as far as they would go and stood for a while, looking at the parking lot. I pulled out the drawers in the dresser and found a Bible, three buttons, and a tangle of hair. There was a pencil on the bedside table, and I used it to play tic-tac-toe on the back of my mother's note. With myself. And big deal, I won. I flipped the channels on the TV till I found a *Brady Bunch* rerun, but it was even jitterier and wobblier than *Sesame Street* had been, so I flipped back again.

"Come on, Tommy, let's go," I coaxed again, holding my hand out to him. "There's nothing to *do* in here, and maybe we can find some new stones." I picked up his coffee can and shook it.

He started to rock and stared harder at the spot in back of the television.

I opened the door to the parking lot, propping it back with a chair, and settled down on the step, watching as a cleaning woman in a green-and-yellow muumuu went in and out of the rooms on the other side. I thought about Manda, back in Delaware, and wondered what we would have done on our second day together. If we had had a second day—or a third—a fourth.

After a while Tommy came and sat next to me, holding tight to his can of stones. I waited a bit and then eased it out of his hands, dumping the stones on the ground between his feet. He reached down and swirled them in short choppy swirls until, resting his chin on his knees, he began to separate them, gray on one side and white on the other. We were still sitting there ages later when our mother got back. She gave us a thumbs-up sign and called out, "I found a great apartment in a place called Fair Meadows."

Fair Meadows was just like every other place we'd lived. It had the same already-furnished spindly chairs and lumpy mattresses and dressers with drawers that stuck. The same curled-up linoleum in the kitchen and streaky tiles in the bathroom, and dishes with stains of I-didn't-want-to-know-what on the insides. It wasn't *fair*, and it wasn't a *meadow*.

"But it's home," Mom said, helping me get the yellow suitcase onto one of the beds in the room that was going to be Tommy's and mine. "We'll brighten it up a bit, maybe get some new curtains. I might even paint some baby animals on the wall for Tommy."

"Baby animals?" I said, rolling my eyes to let her know what I thought of that idea. "Even Tommy's too old for that." I could've saved my breath because next thing I knew she'd grabbed a marker and was sketching in a fat bunny rabbit with sticking-up ears on the wall behind the beds.

"Mom—don't. You can't."

"I just did," she said. We went back through the living room on our way to get more stuff out of the car, detouring around Tommy, who was sitting in the middle of the floor.

"He's really upset," I said. "I mean *really*."

"Oh, he'll be fine. My Tommy's a tough one, right, Tom?" said Mom. "Anyway, moving's a bit of a pain for everyone."

"But he's not like everyone," I said. "And he shouldn't have to do this. He ought to be able to stay put. He ought to be able to have friends and go to school. And he ought to be able to go to a doctor if that's what he needs—to see what's *wrong* with him."

My mother's hand was so fast, I didn't see it coming. It caught me on the side of the head and made my eyes water. "Ought, ought, ought," she said. "If it's not 'what if,' it's 'ought.' Maybe *you* ought to think of that next time, before you start messing around with strangers. If you're so set on our not having to move again. Now help me get the rest of the things out of the car."

We finished the unloading in silence. Once we were done, she said, "There's a sub shop around the corner. Why don't you run over and pick us up some lunch? Plain turkey with no mayo for Tommy, but get what you want for the two of us. Surprise me, okay?" I shivered and pulled back as she reached out to touch me on the side of the head. "Okay?" she said, handing me a twenty-dollar bill.

"Yeah, I guess," I said.

I was partway to the door when Mom called, "Oh, and Elsie, after lunch I have to go out and find a bank and then start looking for a job. We don't want to spend any more of the May money than we have to."

The May money is the money my mother inherited from her great-aunt May ages back before I was born. It's a sort of nest egg and windfall all rolled into one, and it's what we use when Mom doesn't make enough waitressing. Sometimes I wish Great-aunt May had left the money to the poor or the SPCA or something. I mean, maybe if she hadn't had it, my mother wouldn't have been able to kidnap Tommy and me from our father.

There was a sign with the words HASSIE'S SUBS and a picture of a cartoon man with bulgy eyes wearing a camouflage hat hanging outside of the shop. Inside, a woman with regular eyes but wearing the same hat was chopping onions as she listened to a twangy kind of music on the radio. She looked up and smiled when I came in.

"Are you Hassie?" I asked.

"More or less. For practical purposes. The original Hassie was my husband, but then he up and died eight months ago and left me with the business. But hey, I figured I worked here alongside of him for twenty-three years, and chances were I could go on another twenty-three on my own. So I put my troubles on my head and slammed Hassie's hat down on top. That's what you do with troubles you can't do anything about—slam something down on top of them."

"What about the others? Other troubles, I mean," I said.

"You fix them. Do your dang-blasted best to fix them. Now tell me about you. I'm right good about never forgetting a face, and I don't think I've seen you in here before."

The skin on the back of my neck started to prickle, but before I could think of what to say, the woman held her hand out to me saying, "I'm Vi—Violet Hassie—and you are?"

"Elsie," I said. And all of a sudden there was a pop-up thought in my head. What would happen if I said, *I'm Linda Clay McGee and I don't belong here.*

"Elsie who?"

"McPhee."

"Well, Elsie McPhee, welcome to Hassie's Subs. I'm right pleased to make your acquaintance. You and your family settling in around here?"

"I guess," I said, staring hard at the list of sandwiches on the wall in back of Vi.

"New to Richmond? There's a lot of history around these parts. Get your mama or daddy to take you to the Museum of the Confederacy, or the capitol building. Where'd you all live before this?"

I shrugged and looked down at the floor, but before I could think of what my mother would want me to say, Vi was going on. "Too many questions, right? Hassie used to fuss with me about that. 'Violet,' he'd say, 'folks come in here for lunch or supper, not an interrogation.' And I reckon he was right. Tell you what, we'll make a deal. I won't ask you questions, and you won't ask me. *Except* you are allowed to ask me what's the best sub in the whole place. Got it?"

"Got it," I said. "What *is* the best sub in the whole place?"

"The Shoot the Works." She pointed to a red and white sign on the back wall. "Can't beat it."

"All right," I said. "I'd like two of those, please. And then I want one plain roll with plain turkey and no mayo or mustard or pickles or anything else."

"*Bor*-ing," said Vi as she took three rolls out of a package. "Who's that for? Oops, forget I asked that. Okay, two Shoot the Works and one—whatever."

Vi's hands seemed to fly as she piled roast beef and turkey and cheese, tomatoes and shredded lettuce, black olives and onions on two of the rolls, then squirted mayo and mustard and a bunch of other things on top. She wiped her hands and carefully laid pieces of turkey on the other one before wrapping each sandwich in foil.

"Here you go, Miss Elsie McPhee," she said, taking my money and handing me the change. "And you come back real soon, even if it's just for a visit. We're partial to visiting around these parts, you hear that?"

"Okay, and thanks," I said. I stopped outside and looked back in, but Vi was already busy with another customer, so I turned instead and waved to the original Hassie on the sign overhead.

Back at the apartment, Mom had set the table with mismatched plates and made instant iced tea except there wasn't any ice. On account of the trays were still sitting on the sink. "Was the shop okay?" she asked. "Clean and all?"

"I guess. I didn't pay much attention. It's just a sub

shop." I swallowed back the things I wanted to be able to tell someone about Vi and how she'd piled her troubles on her head and slammed Hassie's camouflage hat on top. About how she told me to come back soon, and that troubles that *could* be fixed *should* be fixed.

"Looks good," my mother said, unwrapping her Shoot the Works. "Let's eat."

Mom left after lunch to go to the bank and to maybe look for a job, and I went into our bedroom and started unpacking the yellow suitcase, shoving Tommy's stuff in the bottom two drawers and mine in the top. Not even trying to smooth away the wrinkles. When I was done, I stowed the suitcase in the back of the closet and sat on the edge of my bed, allowing myself to think back to that other day.

Tommy and I hadn't had any clothes, except the ones we were wearing, the day our mother snatched us from off the playground. The morning after we got to New Jersey she took us shopping, and the weird thing was, she tried to make it into some kind of big-deal adventure. We went to Kmart and Wal-Mart and a bunch of other marts. We bought Mickey Mouse T-shirts and shorts and jeans. We bought socks and toothbrushes and underwear, and even a pack of underpants for me with the days of the week sewn in squiggly letters across the fronts.

Mom got us hot dogs from a cart on the street, but she must have forgotten that Tommy didn't like mustard, or hot dogs either, because he howled when she handed him his and threw it on the ground for the pigeons to peck at. After that she went back to the cart and got him a plain empty roll. Tommy sat down on the sidewalk, tearing that roll into little bits, eating some and lining up the rest on the sidewalk in front of him. The pigeons ate those, too.

When lunch was done, Mom had said, "Come on," pointing to the store where we'd gotten the days-of-the-week underpants. That was something else she must have forgotten about Tommy: that sometimes when you tell him to do something, he doesn't. Anyway, Mom said, "Come on" again, this time in a sharp do-it-now voice. She reached out for him, but my brother curled himself into a blob, sort of like a slug there on the sidewalk.

"Come on, Tommy. Right this minute. I'm not fooling," my mother said.

The slug on the sidewalk got tighter and smaller. Several people stopped to watch. "What's wrong with the kid?" said a man leaning on a bicycle.

"There's *nothing* wrong with him," my mother snapped, shoving her hands into her hair. Then she turned to me and whispered, "Do something with him, Elsie. I'll meet you both inside."

I waited for her to be all the way gone before I sat

down on the ground next to Tommy, trying to pretend we were in our own backyard and that people weren't having to move around us to get where they were going. I hummed and talked a kind of monotonous gobbledygook. I made pigeon noises, and after a while I took Tommy by the arm and steered him into the store.

Mom was waiting by a display of window fans, and as soon as she saw us she led us into the women's bathroom. She rooted through her shopping bags, pulling out clothes for each of us, and before Tommy had a chance to sit down or fold up, she peeled his shirt off and put a clean one on. "Here, Elsie, change everything, and get into some of your new things," she said.

"Not here," I said. "Not in public."

"It's not public, for heaven's sake. Do you see anybody here but us?"

"Well, there could be," I said.

"Go in there then," she said, pointing to one of the stalls, "but make it snappy. I'm going to take you to the library, and I don't want to keep company with a couple of ragamuffins."

I opened one of the doors and went in, hanging my new clothes on a hook and struggling to keep from falling into the toilet as I got out of my old stuff and into the Tuesday underpants, denim shorts, and a Mickey Mouse shirt. I went back out into the room, and as soon as Mom saw me, she grabbed my old clothes, bunched them together with Tommy's, and shoved them into the trash can.

"Mom, stop! They're our things." I reached into the can to try to get them, but she pulled me away and led me over to the sink, saying, "They're gone, so leave them be. Besides, all that's done with now." She held my hands out and squirted a blob of slimy pink soap onto them. "Wash yourself, Elsie. No telling what was in that trash can."

I washed my hands and rinsed them and then stood staring as the soapsuds swooshed around the sink. And it was as though my whole past went down the drain along with them.

6

My mother found a job in Richmond that first day she went out looking for one. It was at the Purple Plum Vegetarian Delight, which to me sounded a lot like working in a garden filled with bowers and baskets and trailing vines. Maybe even a waterfall. But when I said that to her, she laughed and said, "The only waterfall at the Purple Plum is the waitresses filling the water glasses. It's mostly high-priced lettuce, but I think the tips'll be good."

The odd thing, though, was the way she totally wigged out when I asked when she was going to show us the restaurant. "You always take us to where you work, at least some of the time. Remember the french fries at the Nifties Fifties and how that waitress in New Jersey gave us brownies with ice cream on top?" I said.

"Not this time," Mom whispered, as if there was someone other than Tommy and me who might be listening. "The vibes aren't right. And besides, I think they could be watching."

"Who? Watching what?"

"Never you mind," she said. "Just stay safe."

"How can I not be safe? We never go anywhere or do anything to be *un*safe."

"What do you expect? We just got here," Mom said. "I just found a job and we've barely settled in."

"But we never do, no matter what. Go anywhere, I mean." I suddenly felt as if the walls of the apartment weren't big enough to hold me. I remembered the places Vi had told me about the day before, and without thinking I blurted out, "Why can't we go to the Museum of the Confederacy or the Capitol or someplace. You won't ever let us go to school, so why can't we at least go *there*?"

Mom slammed her pencil and sketch pad down on the table and spun around to face me. "What do you know about the Museum of the Confederacy, or the Capitol, either?" she said. "We've only been in town for two days. Who have you been talking to? I saw some kids on the parking lot yesterday—did you sneak out to play with them after I left to go look for work? Answer me, Elsie, did you?"

"No," I said. "No." Thoughts swirled around me, and I heard myself saying, "The bus. It was on the side of a bus yesterday, when we were in the car coming from the motel to here. There was this humongous sign all along one side, and it said 'Visit the Museum of the Confederacy and the Capitol' in big red letters. I swear."

"You'd better not be lying to me," my mother said, her eyes that a minute ago had been wide and fiery now small and squinty.

"How could I be lying?" I said, not even bothering to cross my fingers. "We never go anywhere for me to see *people*."

My mother turned away from me and picked up her pad and pencil, concentrating on the picture of Tommy in front of the television she had been working on. Except that in the drawing Tommy's eyes were open instead of halfway closed and the TV was on instead of off. After a few minutes, she looked up again and sighed. "Okay, come on," she said. "Let's go to the library. Get your shoes on, Tommy."

You'd think my mom would know by now that if she said "Get your shoes on, Tommy," he wouldn't. But anyway we went through the regular hassle. Mom found the shoes. She put them on the floor in front of him. She waited. She tapped her foot. That's when I took a deep breath and held it, counting to see how long before she'd say, "You help him, Elsie." And when she did say it, I mouthed the words along with her.

"Is the library far?" I asked once we were outside and my mother was heading for the car.

"Not really," she said. "I saw it yesterday. It's across

the street and up a ways, then off to the left."

"Let's walk then. Tommy needs exercise—he's getting blobby. And I need exercise, too." With that I dug the toe of my sneaker into the parking lot and pushed myself off, running full-speed across the blacktop and the scriggle-scraggle lawn of Fair Meadows, along the sidewalk to the corner. I leaned against a newspaper box, panting and waiting for my mother and brother.

Across the street, we went past a dry cleaner's and a shoe repair shop, past a grocery store and a copy center. Just as we got to Hassie's Subs, the door opened and Vi came out, carrying a squeegee and a bottle of Windex. She looked straight at me as she said, "Hey there, off for a walk?"

Don't let her say any more, I willed. *Don't let her ask how we like Richmond or who ate the turkey-whatever on the plain roll. Or say how she never forgets a face and when am I going to stop in for a visit. Don't let her.* I clenched my fingers and turned my head the other way.

I heard my mother say, "Hello." I felt her shiver as she put one arm around me and one around Tommy, pulling us close. We walked that way a few more blocks, but as soon as we turned onto a side street, I broke away and ran all the way to the library.

Once inside I headed for the children's section to get a copy of *Meet the Austins*, which I've read a million times but keep reading, mostly I guess because it's about the kind of family I'd like to be a part of. From there I went to the young-adult section and got a book I hadn't read yet with a picture on the cover of a girl with spiky hair sitting on a porch and looking at the ocean.

I found my mother and Tommy in the little kids' section. Mom was on the floor with a bunch of Jessie Bear books and the mouse-cookie and moose-muffin books spread out around her. "He should be getting *real* books, with chapters," I said. "And he should be reading them himself."

"Nonsense," Mom said. "I've told you he's fine the way he is. Why can't you see that? Besides, these are his favorites. Right, Tom-Tom?"

Tommy didn't answer her but just kept picking at the tattery edge of a book on the shelf as he stared at a Winnie-the-Pooh poster without really looking at it.

"These will do," my mother said, choosing three books and shoving the rest back on the shelf. She stood up and reached for my books, saying, "Come on, Elsie. I'll go register for a card, and we'll check these out."

"Mom, wait," I said, taking hold of Tommy and trying to catch up with her. By the time we got across the library, she was already next in line. "Wait," I said again. "Why can't I get my own library card this time? I'm tired of you always having to check out my books. Same as I'm tired of you treating me like some wimpy kind of baby. *Everybody* has her own card. Besides, you said I could."

"I never did."

"You did. In Delaware—you said someday."

"And this isn't someday, miss," Mom said. "Someday is when you're all grown up and don't need me to protect you, but since you don't have anyone *else* right now—what do you want to do? Have your name spread all over town, like a sign on a bus? Too much exposure is a dangerous thing." The man ahead of us moved on, and Mom stepped up, putting the books on the counter but keeping one hand on top of them. "I'd like to register for a card," she said.

"Here you go," said the woman behind the desk, sliding a paper over to her. "Just complete this form, please."

My mother filled it out with tall capital letters, then signed her name across the bottom and handed it back. "That's fine," the woman said. "Now I'll need to see a picture ID and something with your name and address on it."

Mom took her driver's license out of her wallet and put it on the counter. I looked at it for a minute, wondering for the first time ever how she got a license that said Jude McPhee instead of Julie McGee, and thinking how Julie had disappeared along with Timmy and Linda Clay. The library clerk picked the license up and looked at it, shaking her head and saying, "But this is from Delaware. I need something with your current address."

"We just moved here the day before yesterday," my mother said. "From Delaware. What do you people think—that I carry a copy of my lease along with me? We're right over at Fair Meadows anyway."

"I'm sorry, Ms. McPhee," the woman said. "But it's a library regulation."

"What is going on here?" my mother said. "Is it some kind of conspiracy? Someone checking on us?" Her voice grew tight and almost shrill.

Tommy sat on the floor and began to rock, making a humming noise that turned into a moan.

I put my hands up to my ears and took a step back, and then another and another. I bumped into a chair and turned and ran to the far end of the library, trying not to hear my mother or my brother. I looked up and saw that I was standing in front of a giant bulletin board, and I stared at it as hard as I could, reading posters and schedules of classes, notes about lost dogs and drum lessons and apartments for rent.

All the way down at the bottom, on one side, was a blue-and-white card with the words HAVE YOU SEEN US? printed on it. There was a picture of a girl named Sarajane and a short description of what she looked like and how long she'd been missing. Next to her was a picture of a woman I guessed was her mother.

Missing missing missing. The word throbbed inside my head. I blinked my eyes, and Sarajane disappeared and Elsie and Tommy took her place. *Missing.* Someone was looking for Sarajane. There was a number to call in case you found her. *Missing missing missing.* I blinked again, and Sarajane was back. Then I had an idea— maybe someone was looking for me. Maybe someone was looking for Tommy and me.

I glanced over my shoulder to make sure no one was watching, then I took the card off the board, folded it in half, and shoved it deep into my pocket.

7

"It's a public library, and I'm a part of the public," Mom said as she led the way out of the building and down the walk. "I don't see why these people have to make things so difficult. What do they think— that I'm going to make off with their precious books?"

I trailed after my mother, holding on to Tommy's hand and thinking about the library books we'd left on the table in the apartment in Delaware, and how the librarian there probably thought we *had* made off with them. Unless some Good Samaritan type took them back.

"Mom, wait," I said, stopping next to a bike rack and tugging on Tommy to keep him from sitting in the dust. "We *have* to have books. There's nothing to do at Fair Meadows. There's not even anything to do in Richmond, and you'll be going to work and I'll be there with Tommy and—"

"What do you mean there's nothing to do in

Richmond?" My mother turned and came back to where Tommy and I were standing. "We just got here. I don't know what you expect. We'll do things—we'll go to that museum you saw advertised, or to a movie, or maybe a park—soon as I get a chance to check these places out, to make sure they're really safe. And I go to work because that's my job. It'd be nice if I could just sit home and draw pictures all day—pictures that somebody would buy—but remember, I'm all you have. *Your* job is to take care of Tommy." She turned and walked away so that I had to hurry after her to catch the rest of what she was saying. "And we will have books. I'll go back to the library on my way to work, and I'll take that lease and put it right down on the desk in plain sight so that everybody there can see that I am who I say I am."

But you're not who you say you are. Same as Tommy and I are not who you say we *are, either.* The words roared through my head as we followed her to the corner, and I had to concentrate to keep from saying them out loud.

"We passed a grocery store along here, and I want to stop in and get a few things," Mom said. "I know we need milk and lunch meat and apples and OJ—anything else?"

"Pretzels and macaroni-and-cheese," I said. "And maybe chocolate-chip-cookie-dough ice cream—to make Tommy think things here are the same as they were in Delaware."

We stopped in front of the store, and Tommy collapsed onto a bench and straight away locked his arms across his chest and started to rock. "I'll go in by myself, and you stay here with him," my mother said. "It'll be quicker that way."

It wasn't a very large store—not a supermarket, I mean—and I watched through the window until Mom got a cart and disappeared behind a mountain of stacked-up cases of Diet Coke. I looked at Tommy, who was moaning a monotonous moan as he rocked. I looked next door at Hassie's Subs, then back at Tommy. Then, sort of on their own, my legs made a dash for the sub shop, and I yanked the door open and went inside.

"Well, well, well, well," said Vi, resting her fingers on the counter and peering at me from under Hassie's hat. "I thought sure that was you going by a while back, but then when you didn't speak—"

"Sometimes I can't," I said all in a rush. "I just can't. Only I didn't want you to think—you know, that I was snooty or something."

Vi squinted her eyes and looked at me for a long time, finally shaking her head and saying, "Noooo, I'd never take you for snooty. Or snobby or snotty, either. Is everything all right, though?"

"Yeah, fine," I said. "Anyway, you promised—remember? That you wouldn't ask."

"I did, didn't I?" she said. "But sometimes—and

Hassie used to get after me for this—sometimes I have to bite my tongue to keep from asking what I shouldn't ought to ask."

"Please," I whispered, my voice disappearing into the voices coming from the radio behind the counter.

"Tell you what," said Vi. "I'll stick to my part of the bargain if you keep in mind that sometimes things need to be said out loud. Maybe even to change. And remember, I'm most always here, and so long as these feet hold up, I'll be wearing them. Now scoot on out of here before you get a crick in your neck from looking over your shoulder."

Tommy was sitting where I'd left him, still rocking, still moaning, and I flopped down next to him, settling back and trying to look as though I'd been there all along. When Mom came out, she handed me one of the plastic grocery bags and we started home. I felt something cold hitting against my leg and said, "They had it?"

"Had what?"

"Chocolate-chip-cookie-dough."

"They sure did," said Mom. "A whole half gallon, and you and Tommy can have some after supper tonight, while I'm at work. But listen, Elsie, no going outside. No opening the door to strangers." She stopped for a minute, switching her bag to the other hand and saying, in a voice that had gone from ice-cream nice to

70

sharp and stinging, "That's all there are in Richmond—strangers—because we don't know anybody. And let's make sure we keep it that way."

Mom left after lunch, promising to stop at the library on her way to work and double-promising to find me a book—provided the librarian didn't give her a hard time about getting a card. I turned on the TV for Tommy, flipping through soaps, *Teletubbies*, a cooking show. He sat on the floor looking away from the set and resting his head on the couch. He started to whimper.

"Look, Tom-Tom, a cooking show. Want to turn around and see what that lady's making? Watch how she cracks the eggs all with one hand. Maybe it's going to be a cake with mile-high frosting—the kind you like."

Tommy crawled up onto the couch, curling his body into a ball and facing the back cushion. His breathing grew thick and raspy, and I went over to see if he was asleep and stood looking at him for a minute. His face was flushed, and there was a dribble of spit under his mouth. I stayed that way, half-watching my brother and half-watching the lady on the TV until I moved over to the table, sat down, and reached into my pocket.

HAVE YOU SEEN US? I flattened the blue-and-white card out in front of me and traced my fingers over the words. There were pictures of a girl with pigtails and of a woman in glasses, and there were little blobs of blue writing under each of them. I read the girl part aloud first, whispering to keep from waking Tommy.

> *Name: Sarajane Jeffers*
> *Family Abduction*
> *DOB: 9/17/93 Age: 7*
> *Ht.: 30" (at age 3) Wt.: 37 lbs. (at age 3)*
> *Hair: brown Eyes: brown*
> *Sex: F Date missing: 11/2/96*
> *From: Salt Lake City, Utah*

Next I read the writing under the woman's picture.

> *Last seen with: Lillian Jeffers*
> *DOB: 3/13/65 Age: 35*
> *Ht.: 5'7" Wt.: 125 lbs.*
> *Hair: blond Eyes: brown*
> *Sex: F Date missing: 11/2/96*
> *From: Salt Lake City, Utah*

I studied the two pictures, looking from Sarajane to Lillian, as if I was working on a puzzle. I figured that DOB meant "date of birth" and that Lillian was Sarajane's mother. I half-closed my eyes, trying to imagine what the child would look like now, and asking myself a bunch of questions I couldn't answer. Did the mother still have long floppy hair, or had she cut it short and maybe dyed it black, or even red? Was Sarajane just like me, and had Lillian taken her and disappeared, and where were they now? Was Sarajane trapped in an apartment while her mother went to work? And who took care of her? Did she go to a real school?

But most of all I wondered who was left at home and searching for them. A father? Grandparents? A bunch of cousins and aunts and uncles and maybe a dog? And would they ever find them? I looked at the rest of the card, reading the telephone number and the website, by this time not even caring if I woke Tommy. Then the words and pictures blurred before my eyes, and in their place I saw *another* card.

I saw my picture, and Tommy's, and Mom's. I saw our names—L.C. (Linda Clay) McGee and Timmy McGee—and blobs of blue writing telling how old we were and what we looked like and that we were last seen with Julie McGee in Baltimore, Maryland.

A thought popped up in my head, and I remembered the way my father used to whistle a special secret whistle for me every night when he got home from work, and how he kept it up until I ran down the steps to meet him. I remembered how, if I ever hid from him, when we were in the kitchen making popcorn or getting ready to go for a walk, Dad would sing, in his Glinda-from-the-Wizard-of-Oz voice, "Come out, come out, wherever you are—" And I remembered how, after he found me, he'd always swing me up high and say, "I don't like it when I can't find you—even if it is a game."

Was my father really looking for Tommy and me? Had he been looking all this time? Was there a blue-and-white card out there with our pictures on it? Did people read it and throw it in the trash? Did anyone ever look at it and say, "I saw those people in the library," or, "They were at the store"?

And was that why my mother never wanted us to go anywhere?

The Sarajane card came back into focus, and I lightly touched the telephone number of where to call if you had seen her. What would happen if I could somehow manage to go out and call it? Would they know about me? About Tommy? Or would they just hang up? Then I thought about my mother and how I was never allowed to go anywhere and how maybe that was the real reason we never had a phone.

I remember Mom saying that Dad didn't want Timmy and me anymore, that she was doing him a favor by taking us away. A torrent of memories swept over me, and I had to bite my lip to keep from crying out that it wasn't true. I could hear the way my father's voice used to sound when he read *The Wind in the Willows* to me and almost taste the pancakes he sometimes made on Saturdays. I thought of Nana and Popoo and how they took me to the aquarium and the science center where they had the giant movie that sort of made me feel sea-sick. For a minute I could almost feel my cat, Tiger, as he rubbed against my legs, but when I put my hand down, there was nothing there.

"Maybe I *could* get some money and go out to a phone booth and call our old number," I said to myself. But when I tried to remember the number, twos and sevens and sixes and nines jumbled in my head. Then I thought of what Mom had said the day she stole us away—that Dad would move out of our house, that Nana and Popoo wanted to travel. And how she had called from the pizza place and nobody had answered.

I looked at the card again and knew that the *www* thing was a website, but we didn't have a computer. I also knew there was no way my mother would let me loose in the library long enough to do what you were supposed to do to find it. Besides, who could I trust to teach me?

I remembered the times my mother had said that she was all we had in the whole world, and suddenly, even with Tommy asleep on the couch nearby, I felt more alone than I ever had before. I folded the card and put my head down on top of it, promising myself I wouldn't cry.

Tommy slept all afternoon, and when he awoke he was crabby, and after a bit he gave up moaning and started to cry. Somehow I got him over to the table, but when I put a grilled cheese sandwich down in front of him, he pushed it onto the floor. I fixed him a serving of chocolate-chip-cookie-dough ice cream and set it on the table, holding tight to the bowl. "Come on, Tommy, here's your favorite," I coaxed. "Mom bought it special for you. Try a little."

Tommy looked at the ice cream. He reached his spoon out and took a little and put it in his mouth, but when he went to swallow it, he cried harder and turned away. He got down on the floor and crawled over to the couch. I sat beside him, putting my hand on his forehead, which was burning hot, and singing the little-teapot song he sometimes liked. And after a while he fell asleep again.

I sat watching my brother and listening to him breathe until it was almost time for Mom to get home from work. Then I went into my bedroom and peeled off my clothes, taping the blue-and-white card to my skin before I put on my pajamas. That was because sometimes, when my mom gets really spooked, she hunts through all the drawers and cupboards—to make sure no one is after us.

I wrote, "Tommy's sick," in red crayon on a piece of paper, propped it against the toaster oven in the kitchen, and went to bed.

8

"Up, Tommy, up. Come on, let's get moving."
Mom's voice was both cheery and cross when it bur-
rowed into my sleep and finally woke me. As if she'd
been saying the same thing for a very long time.

"Mom, he's *sick*," I said, pushing myself up onto my
elbow. "Didn't you get my note last night?"

"I got it, but of course he isn't sick. My Tommy never
gets sick. Besides, when I moved him from the couch to
his bed, he didn't *say* he was sick. Now, I have to work
the lunch shift today, and it's beautiful and warm outside. Let's not waste this time. Up, Tommy, up."

"Tommy doesn't say anything much about *anything*,"
I said as I sat on the edge of my bed and watched as she
struggled to get my brother into a sitting position. His
face was flushed, and his eyes, only half open, were
oozing gunk. He wobbled there for a minute, then
pulled away, falling back onto the mattress and rolling
toward the wall.

"All right, Elsie, you deal with him," said Mom, turning to the door. "The two of you come in for breakfast. I told you, I don't want to waste this wonderful spring day, and I have to leave here by eleven. Now get moving."

I blinked and stretched, thinking how spring had gotten Mom all fired up this morning. She usually brags that the early bird is welcome to all the worms that are out there—that *she's* not a morning person. Moving over to the other bed, I felt Tommy's head, and it was hotter than it had been the night before. While I was in the bathroom, I soaked a washrag in cold water and brought it back, holding it over my brother and squeezing it. He didn't even flinch when the water ran down his face and onto the pillow. I pulled the sheet over his shoulder and went to find my mother.

"Well? Did you get him up?" she asked, putting down her coffee.

"He's *sick* and he can't get up. I told you last night, and I'm telling you this morning," I said.

"And I told you—Tommy never gets sick. Watch your tone of voice, missy."

"I don't see what's the big deal about my tone of voice when you don't even care that your own son is sick."

"If Tommy were really sick, I would care," Mom said. "But you know yourself, he doesn't always want to do what we want him to do. It's one of his little quirks."

"They're *not* quirks," I cried. "There's something wrong with him, and anybody can see that. But right now he's sick, too. He didn't eat his grilled cheese last night, and he didn't eat his chocolate-chip-cookie-dough ice cream, and that's his absolute favorite. And besides, he was crying, and even with all that moaning Tommy hardly ever cries real tears. And besides *that*, his forehead is burning hot."

Mom pushed her empty mug aside and stood up, looking at me through little slitty eyes. "Don't ever say anything like that again. Tommy has quirks, harmless quirks. We all have them," she said. "But if it will make you happy, I'll give him some of that children's Tylenol I got last year when you had the flu." She found the bottle in the cabinet and took a spoon off the counter, heading toward the bedroom. I was halfway through my cereal when she came back.

"I couldn't get him to wake up enough to take it," she said. "He must be really zonked. Did you let him stay up too late last night?"

"No. I told you, Tommy's sick, and all he did yesterday was sleep from the time you left till now, except for the little while I got him to the table when he wouldn't eat."

"Well, you can try to give him some Tylenol later," my mother said, "only it's pretty obvious that if he really needed it, he would have taken it. The body knows what the body needs."

I took a deep breath to keep my voice from wobbling, and staring down at my bowl, I said, "He's sick, and he needs to go to a doctor."

"What did you say?" my mother said.

"That he needs to go to a doctor!" This time I shouted it out.

"Don't be ridiculous. Doctors don't do anything but ask a lot of questions and snoop into matters that don't concern them. You can never trust them, what with their poking and probing and putting the worst possible spin on things. What do you think—that they're some kind of gods? Well, they're not, and I'll tell you one thing flat out, Miss Elsie McPhee, my Tommy is not seeing any doctor." My mother took her coffee mug and slammed it into the sink, then turned back to face me. "I'm getting out of here. I'd rather be early for work than stand around and listen to this nonsense. Maybe I'll work lunch *and* dinner."

And almost before I knew what was happening, she had grabbed her keys and purse and was out the door.

I waited until I heard the car pull away before I grabbed the bottle of medicine and headed for Tommy's and my room. Peeling back the sheet and rolling him over to get his face out of the pillow, I started talking in a singsong voice. "Come on now, Tommy. I need for you to sit up and take this nice medicine on account of it's going to make you feel better, and then you'll be able to get out of bed and play with your stones and watch TV, and you can even have some chocolate-chip-cookie-dough ice cream. There's a whole ton more in the freezer."

I shoved both of our pillows under his head, read the label on the bottle, and poured out a spoonful. "Come on, Tom-Tom. Open wide." I forced the spoon into the corner of his mouth, and the medicine disappeared, then suddenly reappeared. I scraped it off his chin and shoved it in again. "There you go, that's a good boy," I said as I poured another spoonful and pushed that one in, too. I turned to put the bottle on the table and turned back just in time to see Tommy open his mouth and a great gush of medicine run out and down onto his shirt. He looked at me as if he'd never seen me before, then his eyes rolled up into his head and he slipped off the pillows and onto the mattress.

I wiped his face with a damp washrag, but when I tried to change his T-shirt, his arms seemed to be made of rubber and I gave up. Sitting on the edge of my own bed, I watched his chest go up and down and listened to his breathing, which came in short, choppy spurts. After a while I went into the living room and watched the clock. The day stretched out ahead of me.

My mother had gone to work, and I didn't know when she would be home.

My brother was sick, and there was nothing I could do.

Mom said no doctor was going to see her Tommy.

"But he's my Tommy, too," I said out loud as a whole string of what-ifs spun through my head. I got up and went back in the bedroom to watch my brother breathe some more.

I thought about giving Tommy another spoonful of medicine, but I was afraid to. I mean, what if he had swallowed some of the first dose and then I gave him more and then what would happen? What would happen if I *didn't* give him any more? I went into the living room to look out the window, as if I'd been expecting someone to be waiting there—to tell me what to do. I remembered the girl Manda who had moved into the A building in Delaware. I remembered her mother with the spiky hair, and her father, and her brother. They would help me—I was sure of it. If they were here or we were there.

I went back to the bedroom again and put my hand on Tommy's forehead and quickly pulled it away. I shook him and called his name, but he didn't respond. His raspy breathing was the only sound in the room.

Back in the living room, I wished, more than anything, that we had a phone so I could call my mother at the Purple Plum Vegetarian Delight. But even as I was thinking this, I shook my head. I knew Tommy needed help. I also knew my mother wouldn't get it for him.

Somebody has to and there's only me and I don't know

anybody. Thoughts raced through my head, and I remembered how Mom had said that Richmond was full of strangers. And how she wanted to keep it that way. "We haven't even been anywhere to see anybody," I whispered, "except the library and the store, only I sat outside, and the sub shop." All of a sudden the sign with the cartoon person in the camouflage hat and the words *Hassie's Subs* flashed before my eyes. I could almost hear Vi saying, "So long as these feet hold up, I'll be wearing them."

I ran back to the bedroom, sitting on the side of Tommy's bed and taking hold of his hot, dry hands. "Tommy, listen. I've got to tell you this." I knew he couldn't hear me, but I had to tell him anyway.

"We've got to get help on account of you're really sick, only Mom says you're not and that you don't need anything. Except you do. And I couldn't figure what to do, but now I've thought of something. Of someone. Her name is Vi and she works at this sub shop and she's really nice and she said that sometimes things need to be talked about and maybe even to change." I stopped for a minute and looked at my brother, who had pulled his hands away and rolled onto his side.

"And I know she'll help, and she'll—" I stopped, not exactly sure what it was that I expected Vi to do. Would she come right away and take Tommy to a doctor, or maybe a hospital? Would she call an ambulance, or maybe bring a nurse? Or would she—and here the floor seemed to shake under my feet—would she find our father and send him to get us?

I reached under my T-shirt and unstuck the blue-and-white card from my skin where I'd put it the night before. "I've got to do something," I said to Tommy, but mostly to myself. "I've got to go someplace and do something, and then I'll be right back, and while I'm gone you'll be by yourself, but I promise I'll run all the way." I moved over to my own bed, pushing the lamp on the night table aside and flattening the blue-and-white card out in front of it. Drawing a line from the HAVE YOU SEEN US? question, I wrote, "L.C. (Linda Clay) and Timmy McGee only now we're Elsie and Tommy McPhee are with Jude McPhee who used to be Julie McGee." I read over what I had written and carefully printed the name of our apartment complex in Richmond and added the apartment number. Then, picking up a red marker, I wrote, "Tommy's really sick. Please help us."

I shoved the card down deep in my pocket and dropped the string with the apartment key on it over my head. But I couldn't leave. All of a sudden I had turned into a robot, moving back and forth between Tommy's bed and the front door. Back and forth, back and forth. On what had to be maybe my twenty-millionth trip, I hung over my brother, trailing my fingers across his forehead and whispering, "I've got to do it, Tom-Tom. I've got to get us help, but I'll be fast. I swear to you."

Then I turned and ran, through the apartment and out the door, pulling it tight behind me and heading over the parking lot to the scruffy grass of Fair Meadows and onto the sidewalk. Without even stopping for breath, I started out into the street, just as a giant truck swerved and screeched and skidded to a stop and a red-faced man leaned out of the window, shaking his fist at me. "What're you trying to do, kid, get yourself killed?"

I jumped back onto the curb, wrapping my arms around a lamppost and listening to my heart pounding in my chest. Trying not to think about Tommy home all alone—and that I had almost been run over. I took a deep breath and then another, and another, finally letting go of the lamppost and watching for a break in the traffic. I dashed across the street and down past the dry cleaner's and the shoemaker's and the little grocery store where Mom had gotten the chocolate-chip-cookie-dough ice cream that Tommy didn't eat. The sign for Hassie's Subs loomed up ahead, and I ran even faster, pushing at the door and almost falling into the shop.

The radio was playing a bumpety kind of song. Two women and a man were standing at the counter talking to Vi as she wrapped a bunch of subs in aluminum foil. But I couldn't wait and without thinking I wormed my way in front of the man and said, "Please. You've got to help. It's my brother Tommy, and he's really sick and I've left him alone so I've got to get back." I dug the card out of my pocket and shoved it across the counter to her. "Please," I said again as I turned and ran out of the store.

I raced all the way home, stooping to unlock the door without even taking the key from around my neck, and hurried into Tommy's room. He hadn't moved from when I left, and I stood watching him for a minute before collapsing onto my own bed and struggling to catch my breath. "I did it, Tommy," I said. "And now we're just going to have to wait."

After a while I went into the kitchen for a glass of water. The clock on the wall said eleven o'clock.

9

By eleven thirty I was really antsy. I was sitting next to the bed holding tight to Tommy's hand and trying to decide what to do next. "Maybe if I count non-stop to five hundred, something will happen," I told myself. But I did—and it didn't.

"Maybe if I stay away from the window for half an hour, *then* something will happen." But that idea was just taking shape in my head when I jumped up and ran to the front room, knocking my shoulder against the door frame and tripping over a half-full laundry basket to get to the window.

I forced myself to turn away and went, instead, over to the kitchen counter, where I stood staring at a box of Cheerios. "If I don't look out, someone will come. If I just don't look."

But what if no one does? I thought. What if Vi had wanted to call and then found we didn't have a phone? What if the ambulance company had wanted to call?

What if they had some rule about only going places with telephones? What was Vi doing now? Was she on her way here? Had she been able to get help? Or had she decided it was all a trick and thrown the blue-and-white card with our names and address on it in the trash? What would I do then?

My head pounded and my knees shook as I reached for a chair and sat down. "No," I said out loud. "She wouldn't. And she *will* do something." *But what if she doesn't? What if no one comes? What'll I do then?*

When I looked at the clock again, it was a quarter to twelve and I got up and went back to Tommy's room. "She'll come," I said to him. "I promise you." Tommy groaned and a trickle of spit ran out of the corner of his mouth. His breath smelled sharp and sort of spicy.

I stretched out on my bed and closed my eyes, and for a minute I felt distant and sort of floaty. When I opened my eyes, Tommy was staring at me.

"You're awake," I said, jumping up. "Do you want water or ice cream or juice?" I didn't wait to see if he would answer me but headed into the kitchen and came back with a bowl of ice cubes.

"Here you go, try this first," I said, rubbing a cube back and forth along his lips. He kept his mouth shut tight and after a while he closed his eyes and turned his head away.

I sat and watched the ice melt in the bowl, listening

to the rattle of the cubes as I stirred them with my fingers. From somewhere far away I heard a siren and got up and went into the living room, pressing my forehead against the windowpanes, waiting to see what would happen. I blinked and could almost see the ambulance as it pulled onto the parking lot, but when I opened my eyes wide, it wasn't there and the sound of the siren was getting farther and farther away.

There was a gnawing feeling deep in my stomach, and I didn't know whether it was because of the ambulance that didn't come or maybe that I was hungry. I went into the kitchen and made a peanut-butter-and-jelly sandwich and poured a glass of milk, then took them back to the window, where I settled down to wait for something to happen. But nothing did.

It was weird. There I was surrounded by bunches of apartments, but where were the people who lived in them? The fronts of the buildings were blank, the doors closed, the windows staring, with no one going in or out. There were cars on the parking lot, but they were the same ones that had been there all morning. Didn't anyone at Fair Meadows need to go to the store or to a doctor's appointment or the dry cleaner's? Did anyone really live here? Maybe it was like some horror movie on TV where everybody was spirited away—except for Tommy and me—and if I screamed my head off, no one would hear me. Maybe my mother wouldn't even come back.

I finished my sandwich and licked my fingers and ran them around the plate, picking up crumbs. I wasn't hungry anymore, but my stomach still hurt.

Ages later a UPS truck pulled onto the lot and stopped. I crossed my fingers and thought how maybe it was a hoax, like the Trojan Horse or something, and that the whole truck was filled with police who were coming to get us. The driver got out, carrying a large box, and went into a building across the way. A few minutes later he came out and drove away, and my stomach hurt even more.

I pushed myself back from the window. In the kitchen I spooned chocolate-chip-cookie-dough ice cream into a bowl and took it into Tommy's room. I stared at the spoon for a minute, then dug my finger in and rubbed ice cream all over Tommy's lips, like some gloppy kind of lipstick. "Lick it, Tom-Tom," I whispered. "Just lick it off." I scooped up another blob, forcing it between his lips. "You'll starve if you don't have food, and ice cream is food. Eat this, and I'll get you some water." I knew that something bad happened if a person didn't have enough to drink, but I didn't know what it was. And I wasn't sure I wanted to know.

And then Tommy licked his lips. I held my breath and watched. I spread more ice cream on his mouth, and he licked again. Then he coughed a hideous choking cough that seemed to come from his feet all the way up through his body. He rubbed at his mouth with his hands and turned away.

Stretching out on my bed, I picked up the book Mom had gotten me from the library yesterday, when she went back with our lease to get her card. It was *Meet the Austins.* I figured if I read it often enough, I'd somehow get to *be* an Austin. I held the cover up so Tommy could see it (if he had been looking, which he wasn't), and I read out the title and the author's name. I read the front inside-of-the-book-jacket aloud, the part that tells what the story's about, and then went on to read the back flap, about the author. I opened the book and read the title again, and the author, and the publisher, and then the whole long list of other books by the same person. I turned the page and read the small print that gave the date when the book was printed and a bunch of other stuff. And as I read, a giant memory cloud settled overtop of me.

I was a little kid again, sitting on my bed at night, waiting for my father to read to me. I could hear the rumbly tumble of his voice as he read out the title, and author, and all the little bits on the front and back flaps; as he opened the book and read the title and author again, the publisher, and then made his voice go little and squeaky as he read the small print. It was at this point that I always caught hold of his arm and shook it, saying, "The story, Daddy. Read the *story.*"

Then my father would laugh and turn the page. "Once upon a time . . ."

I turned the page in my book and started to read to Tommy. " 'It started out to be a nice, normal, noisy evening . . .' " I read aloud until my voice got tired, and then I read to myself. I hurried through the opening part that I pretty much knew by heart, slowing down when I got to the place when Maggy comes to live with the Austins. I kept on reading till my eyelids began to droop and I felt the book slip out of my fingers. I lay there half asleep and half awake, pretending that I really *was* Maggy (only not as bratty) and that I had gone to live with the Austins forever. Along with Tommy, of course.

I was so far down in my dream that when the knock on the door came, I hardly heard it. It came again, only louder, and by the time I got to the living room, it was sharp and sort of demanding. I peered through the tiny glass hole in the door and saw the squishy-stretchy shape of a man holding something that looked like a wallet. "Elsie McPhee, we're from the FBI, and we've come to help you. Please open the door."

10

Open the door. Open the door. The words beat inside my head. I stepped back, and then, after a minute, leaned forward again. The man was still there. His mouth looked long and twisted as he said, "Elsie, we're here to help you, but we need for you to open the door."

But I can't open it, I thought. My mother always told me not to. "Never open the door" is what she said. "Never open the door unless you know who is on the other side."

I *do* know, I told myself. He said he was from the FBI. That he was here to help us. On account of Vi must have sent him. But he didn't *say* that, didn't mention Vi's name. So what if it's all a trick and he's really a burglar or a murderer or something? *"Never open the door."* My mother's words jangled all around me, and I was frozen in place.

The man knocked again, only this time it was more

of a tap. "Are you and your brother all right?" he said.

My brother. Tommy. Pictures rolled before my eyes of Tommy lying in the bed, his forehead hot to the touch, and him turning his head away. I thought of how he hadn't had anything to eat or drink except for the ice cream I smeared on his lips, and how he didn't answer even when I leaned close and talked right into his face.

I forced my arm to move, watching, as if it weren't a part of me, while my hand unfastened the chain and turned the knob. I pulled the door open.

In person, instead of through the peephole, the man didn't look squishy-stretchy at all but plain and ordinary, in a blue suit with a red-and-gray-striped tie. He was holding his identification card out to me, but when I took it, the words and picture blurred and I shoved it back at him. "My name is Hank Bradley and this is Sema James from Child Protective Services," he said, gesturing to the tall, skinny woman beside him. "We'd like to come in and talk to you."

I stood back to let them in and then closed the door and followed them into the room. "You're not here alone, are you?" the Sema woman asked. "We had word there was another child—your brother?"

I nodded, and then, all in a rush, the words spilled out. "That's Tommy, and he's really sick and he doesn't answer when I talk to him and just turns his head away, and he won't eat or drink anything and his head is burning up, and mostly he just sleeps and my mother said he didn't need to see a doctor only I know he *does* and that's why I had to leave him here and go out and give the message to Vi. At the sub shop."

The woman put her arm around my shoulder and said, "I need to go in and see to your brother, but Mr. Bradley has some questions he wants to ask you—and then you can come on in, too. Is that all right?"

I nodded, the whole time digging my feet into the floor to keep from following her.

"You've been very brave through all this, Elsie. And just remember, you did the right thing," Mr. Bradley said. "Now I'd like to ask you a couple of things. Okay?"

"Okay, I guess, except what if my mother comes back? I mean, she went to work on account of she had the lunch shift at the Purple Plum, but she said she might stay and work dinner, too, only she might not and—" I looked over at the clock and said, "It's three thirty already. And the thing is, I'm not supposed to *talk* to people, any people, or let them in, either." All of a sudden I could feel myself shaking from the inside out.

"I think I understand how you feel," Mr. Bradley said. "We have someone waiting on the parking lot to talk to your mother when she gets home. Now, can you tell me your name?"

I looked at him and was afraid to say anything, thinking that maybe this was a trick question and that if

I gave the wrong answer, he and Sema James would turn around and go out the door, leaving Tommy and me alone. Then I took a deep breath and said, "I'm Elsie McPhee, only a long time ago I used to be L.C. McGee—you know, the letters L and C, and sometimes I was Linda or Linda Clay."

"And your brother was Timmy McGee?" Mr. Bradley asked.

I nodded and said, "And my mother was Julie McGee, only now she's Jude. McPhee."

"How long have you been in Richmond?" he said.

"Just a few days, and before that we were in Delaware and before that in New Jersey—a couple of different places in New Jersey."

"All right now," said Mr. Bradley. "Let's go in to see your brother, and we'll see what we can do for him."

I led the way into the bedroom, catching my breath at the sour yucky smell that filled the air. "I tried to give him ice cream and ice, too," I said, pointing to the bowls. "I gave him Tylenol, only he spit most of it out, and I put water on his head." I sat on the edge of the bed and reached for Tommy's hand.

"You did just fine, Elsie," Miss James said as she put her hand on Tommy's forehead. "Your brother's very sick, though, and we're going to have to get him to a hospital."

Mr. Bradley took a phone out of his pocket, and I

heard him calling for an ambulance. When he hung up, he said, "You'll be coming with us, so maybe you'd better put some of your and Tommy's clothes in a bag while we're waiting for the ambulance."

"And Elsie," Miss James said, "your father is on his way."

"*My father?* My *real* father from, you know, before?" My knees wobbled and gave out, and I sat down on the edge of my bed.

"He's on his way to Richmond now," Mr. Bradley said, "but we have his cell-phone number, and once we find out which hospital we're going to, we'll get in touch with him and tell him to go right there. A lot's been happening since we got that call from Mrs. Hassie."

"You mean Vi? From the sub shop?" I said, my head sort of spinning from all that was going on.

"Yes, Vi from the sub shop," Miss James said. "Now, how about getting your things together. Okay?"

I went into the kitchen, grabbed a bunch of plastic grocery bags from the cupboard, and stood for a moment, staring at the apartment door and wondering what I would do if my mother came in. What *she* would do. What she would *say*. Part of me wanted to peek out the window to see if there really was someone waiting for her there, but the other part of me won. I turned and ran back to the bedroom.

Trying to keep my hands from shaking, I pulled jeans

and socks and underwear and shirts out of the drawers and shoved them into bags. Then I started to unpack what I had packed, making room for Tommy's can of stones in one of the bags.

"What are you doing?" Mr. Bradley asked.

"We've got to take these. Tommy gets really agitated when stuff changes, and maybe having the stones will help. Besides, lining them up with the gray on one side and the white on the other is what he likes to do best. There's something wrong with him," I added, not sure exactly why.

"You mean something wrong with him besides being sick right now, the fever and all?" said Miss James.

"Uh-huh," I said, nodding. "He doesn't hardly talk or look at people when they talk to him or do most *any-thing*. My mom says he does, but I know he doesn't."

"How long has your brother been this way?" Miss James said, rearranging the clothes to make room for the stones in a bag.

I shrugged and said, "I guess forever. Only I sort of remember that when I was little and he was really little, he used to talk and then he stopped. That's when my father started wanting to take him to a special doctor, and my mother kept saying no, and after that they mostly fought, and after *that* they got divorced. Dad waited till everything was settled and he had custody before he made an appointment." I stopped for a minute and then heard myself going on, saying out loud what I'd hardly dared to think: "I'm pretty sure that's why my mom stole us away."

Just at that moment I heard a siren, but instead of the sound getting farther and farther away, as it had before, it seemed to come closer and closer until it was right on top of us. And then it stopped. There was a knock at the door. Mr. Bradley went to answer it, and suddenly the apartment was swarming with people.

A man and a woman, who I figured were from the ambulance, came into the room, moving close to the bed and bending over Tommy. One of them reached to take his pulse while the other pushed up his eyelids and shone a little light into his eyes, first one and then the other.

"Time's a factor here," Miss James said to their backs. "We need to get these kids out of here as soon as possible."

"Got you," the man, or maybe it was the woman, answered her.

With that, Sema James touched me on the shoulder, nodding in the direction of the door, and said, "Let's us wait in the other room, Elsie. And let the paramedics take care of Tommy."

We picked up the bags of clothes, and I started to follow her, but my feet seemed to stop, all on their own, just when I got to the door. I must have said something because the lady paramedic looked up and asked, "Is this your brother? He's going to be fine. We'll take good care of him. I promise."

She smiled, and then my feet started up again and I went the rest of the way into the living room. A couple of minutes later the other paramedic went outside and came back pushing a trundly kind of stretcher thing. He took it into the bedroom, and a few more minutes after that they all three came out. The man pushed the stretcher and the woman half-steered and half-pulled the front end while Tommy was flat out between them, wrapped in a blanket with a strap across his chest.

The ambulance was on the parking lot. The back door was standing open, and it looked like a gigantic mouth waiting to swallow somebody up.

"No. You can't put Tommy in there," I cried. "What's going to happen to him?"

Mr. Bradley and Miss James looked at each other. They looked at the paramedics. "You want to ride along with him?" the lady paramedic said. "You can hold his hand and tell him about the scenery—though you can't actually *see* the scenery from back here. How about it?"

"Okay," I said.

"Sema, you ride along with Elsie, and I'll meet you at the hospital," Mr. Bradley said.

We watched as they flattened the legs on the stretcher and slid it into the ambulance. "Now, you hop in there and sit on that seat right next to him," the paramedic said. "I'll ride in back with you, and Miss James'll get in front."

I climbed into the ambulance, reaching over to pat Tommy, whispering that things were going to be okay. The paramedic got in next to me, and just as she sat down, I saw, over her shoulder, my mother suddenly looming in the doorway. Her eyes were wild and her hair seemed to be flying every which way. As I watched, two police officers came up, one on either side of her, reaching out, pulling her back.

"What are you doing?" I heard her shout. "Did you do this, Elsie? Did you talk to people when I told you not to? Did you? Did you?"

Someone closed the ambulance door, and a short time later we started to move. I put my hands up to my ears to shut out my mother's voice. "For Tommy," I said. "I did it for Tommy."

11

I sat on a lumpy orange chair in the hospital waiting room, next to Sema James, who had just got done telling me I should call her Sema instead of Miss James from now on. I nodded okay but didn't say anymore because right then I wanted to think about my mother and the two police officers and what they were going to do to her. I also wanted to think about my father, who was on his way here, and whether I would recognize him or not. But mostly I wanted to think about Tommy, off somewhere in the emergency room surrounded by a bunch of doctors and nurses he didn't know.

The trouble was, my brain seemed to have turned to mush, and what I ended up thinking about was the toe of Sema's left shoe. I stared at it with all my might, as if it was a big deal or something, and wondered why it was scuffed and the right one wasn't. Did she trip a lot, or walk into lampposts? Kick a football? The thing was, I didn't really *care*, but no matter how hard I tried, I couldn't keep from thinking about that shoe.

I let out a giant sigh and forced myself to look up, to count the tiles in the ceiling.

"Why don't we go find the cafeteria and get something to eat?" Sema said.

"I can't," I said. "Because of Tommy. I've got to be here."

"Okay," said Sema, looking at her watch. "But I saw some vending machines down the hall, and I'm going to check them out."

She got up to leave, which was good because then I couldn't look at her shoe anymore, except after that I just stared at where it had been, at the funny chipped place in the floor. When she came back, she was carrying two cans of Sprite and two packages of peanut-butter crackers. "Here," she said, handing me one of each, "this ought to keep us going."

For a while we sat crunching our crackers and drinking Sprite, and after a bit I figured that maybe I really had been hungry because all of a sudden the mush in my brain turned back to questions. Zillions of questions, racing through my head.

"I need to know about my mother," I said. "I mean, what's going to happen to her? I saw those guys, those policemen, and they had ahold of her. And then what?"

"The officers aren't going to hurt your mother,

Elsie," said Sema, crinkling the wrapper from the peanut-butter crackers into a ball. "They just wanted to make it easier for us to move on, and to get your brother to the hospital."

"But now what? With my mom?" All of a sudden the Sprite and crackers felt as though they'd turned into a cement blob in the middle of my stomach. "What'll they *do* to her?"

"Your mother will be charged with a felony that has to do with the harboring of children by a noncustodial parent for more than thirty days, and taking them out of state," said Sema. "Does that make any sense to you?"

"Sort of," I said. "I know that when my mom and dad got divorced, the judge said we were supposed to stay with my father—"

"That made him the custodial parent, and your mother the *non*custodial parent," Sema said.

"Yeah, and the judge said sometimes my mother'd take us out, like to the zoo or her apartment or someplace, and then she'd drop us off back at home, but then my dad made the doctor's appointment for Tommy, and my mom found out and—"

"And she didn't bring you back one day, right?" asked Sema.

"Not exactly. One time we were already at the playground with Blanche, our baby-sitter, and my mom came and found us there—I was up in a swing and I saw her coming toward us. She said we'd go for ice cream and that Blanche should go on home and she, Mom, would bring us later. Only she never did. Well, the ice cream part was true, but after that we just kept on going. To New Jersey. To Delaware. To—" I started to shake as the memory of the last four years swept over me, and Sema reached out to take my hand.

"It's going to be okay," she said.

"It was scary, and weird too, because all along I knew that things weren't supposed to be the way they were for us, with Mom and Tommy and me running from one place to another and us never going to school or to the doctor for checkups or even seeing regular people, like neighbors and stuff. But for a long time I pretty much didn't remember how it used to be. And then I did, and when Tommy got sick, I knew I had to do something—but I never ever wanted my mom to go to *jail*. Will she now?"

Sema took the two soda cans and put them on the floor between our chairs before she said, "Your mom will be escorted back to Baltimore, either by federal marshals or by someone the state of Maryland sends to get her, and once she's there, there will be a bail review hearing, and after that the chances are good that she'll be released on bail. I can't tell you for sure what will happen next—it will have to be decided in court."

"But what about *now* and up until all that happens?

Will my mother be in jail?"

"You know, Elsie, there are times when, for something good to happen, something bad has to happen along with it. But—"

"Will she?" I asked again.

"Yes," said Sema, turning to face me. "Until all this gets sorted out, your mother will have to be detained."

I sat on my chair feeling sort of like the abominable snowman, all cold and blobby, trying to think and not to think about what Sema had just said. I don't know how long I'd been sitting there that way before I felt her touch me on the leg and heard her say, as if from far away, "Look—here comes the doctor who was working on Tommy. Let's go see what he can tell us."

The doctor was the same one we'd seen when we first got there. He was tall and skinny with a bushy mustache and his name, Dr. Greene, sewn in scriggly letters on the front of his white coat. As he came toward us, he was smiling and rubbing his hands together.

"Your brother's doing just fine," he said, looking at me. "And we'll let you go back to see him in just a few more minutes." He turned to Sema and went on, "Tommy has a nasty throat infection, and he was badly dehydrated. We've started him on antibiotics, and we've got him on IV fluids. He's awake, but he hasn't said anything."

"Tommy doesn't mostly," I said. "Say anything, I mean."

106

"Well, as I said, he's definitely on the mend, and someone will come for you in a little while." Dr. Greene turned and disappeared back through a set of double doors that popped open, as if by magic, when he got close to them.

"Good news, huh?" said Sema as she gathered up the empty Sprite cans and threw them in the trash. "And your father should be here soon, too."

"Yeah, but what if he doesn't know who I am after all this time? What if I don't know *him*?" I said as we settled onto those same lumpy orange chairs. I closed my eyes and tried to remember what my father looked like. I opened them again and looked around the room, stopping to stare at a man sitting on the other side and drinking a cup of coffee. What if *he's* my father? I thought. And he's over there and I'm over here and we don't even know each other? Or what if my father's the guy standing at the desk in the slouchy raincoat, or the one by the water fountain in the baseball cap? "What if?" I said out loud.

"I'm sure you've changed a lot in the past four years," Sema said. "And maybe your dad has, too, though even if you don't—"

A man came in the door from the outside. He had on a yellow windbreaker and glasses, and his curly hair was more brown than blond and sort of shaggy. An older man and woman were just in back of him, and they all three stopped for a minute and then headed for the desk.

"Daddy!" I screamed, and flew up off my chair and tore across the waiting room, hurling myself at him. "You're here. You're here."

"I'm here, L.C.," my father said, and he swooped me up and held me tight. "And Nana and Popoo are here with me."

"I know," I said, as my grandmother and grandfather moved in close, and we were all hugging at once.

When we finally untangled ourselves, Sema was waiting beside me. She held her hand out to my father and said, "Mr. McGee, I'm Sema James from Child Protective Services. We're glad to see you."

After that we had to find a whole bunch of lumpy orange chairs, over by the water fountain, and Popoo fixed them in a circle, and we all sat down, with everybody talking at once.

"I can't believe we've found you," Nana said, patting me on the knee.

"A sight for sore eyes," said Popoo. "Though you must have grown a foot."

"We took off as soon as we heard," said Dad. "Now tell me, how's Timmy?"

"Timmy?" I said. "You mean Tommy. But he's tons better, the doctor said, and in a little while we're going to get to see him."

"Tommy." My father said the name as if we were

holding it in his hand and looking at it all around. "Tommy?"

I tried to explain. "That's what Mom called him ever since—you know—and the thing is that Tommy doesn't always answer or look at you, either, even when you call him by a name he *knows*, so—"

"Got you," said Dad. "Tommy's a fine name. But how about you? What have you been—"

"Elsie, same as before, but spelled out E-l-s-i-e," I said. "Only it doesn't matter about me on account of I know who I am."

"Good girl," said Dad.

"I can't believe we've actually found you, Linda," said Nana, patting me on the knee again.

Just then Mr. Bradley arrived from wherever he had been, and he and my father went into the hall to talk. When they came back, Mr. Bradley held his hand out to me and said, "Everything's squared away on this end, Elsie, and I'm going to turn you over to your father and grandparents now. But Sema will be here awhile longer. You take care, and good luck."

I shook his hand and stood up sort of both at the same time, but when I tried to speak, the words came out small and shaky. "Thank you," I said, trying to swallow past the lump in my throat. "Thank you."

After Mr. Bradley left, we all—my dad and my grandparents and Sema and I—sat back down, only this time we had trouble thinking of things to say.

"Well—" my father said. And then, "Well," again.

Nana patted me on the knee a bunch more times, sighing and saying, "Linda Clay."

Popoo crossed his legs one way and then the other, finally leaning forward and saying, "You remember Sandy, that golden retriever of mine? He'll be glad to see you. Had to drop him off at the kennel on our way here, but when I told him where we were going, he didn't mind a bit. Seemed to know it was important."

"I used to walk him on a red leash," I said, fishing back into my past. "Maybe I could do it again when I get, you know, home."

"He'd like that. Sandy's slowing down some, but he still likes a good long walk. You know something, Linda, I've been thinking maybe I should get a puppy, to keep Sandy company and all. Think you could help me with that?"

Before I could tell Popoo I surely could do that, a nurse came up and said that two of us could go to see my brother. I stood up straight away. My father stood up next to me. He put his hand on my shoulder, and we followed the nurse across the waiting room and through the popping-open doors.

Tommy was lying on a high sort of bed in a tiny room. There was a plastic bag hanging on a pole with a tube going into his hand. His eyes were open, but it didn't look as if anybody was there. He seemed all empty inside.

"Hi Tom-Tom, it's me," I said, moving close and taking hold of the hand without the tube in it. His skin felt cooler and more like real skin. He didn't look at me.

"Tommy?" I said. "Tommy? You're in the hospital, and the doctors and nurses are making you all better. I've got your stones in my bag, and tomorrow when you're feeling really good, you can play with them. Okay?" I leaned over, putting my head right in front of where his eyes were staring, but even then, in some weird way, he still wasn't looking at me.

My father stood next to me, without saying anything. "You've got to talk to him," I said. "You've got to keep talking."

He cleared his throat and said, "Hi, Tommy. I'm your dad, and I'm here now, and your grandmother and grandfather are with me."

"That's Nana and Popoo, Tommy," I said. "Only I don't know if you remember them on account of you were pretty little the last time you saw them. And they have this dog named Sandy, and now Popoo says that maybe he'll get a puppy." I nodded for my father to say something.

"We've been looking for you and L.C. for a long, long time. And now we've found you," he said, his voice thick and husky. "And as soon as you're better, we're going to take you home." He put his finger on my brother's face, but Tommy didn't look at him.

"We're going to get in the car and go to a place where you haven't been since you were really small, but it's okay and you're going to like it there," I said. "I promise you it's going to be okay, and we'll have your stones and you can play with them and we'll find some more. Lots of little ones."

Before either Dad or I could say any more, Tommy started to moan and to rock his head from side to side. My father looked over at me. He raised his eyebrows.

"It's all right," I said. "He does that some."

Dr. Greene came in then. He shook hands with my father and told him what he had told Sema and me before, about Tommy's throat and how he had been dehydrated. "We're going to put him in a regular room upstairs," he went on, "and I'm sure by tomorrow you can take him home."

"That's good to hear," said Dad. Then he turned to me and said, "I'll tell you what. We'll go up with Tommy and see him settled in his room, and then you and your grandparents and I will go to a hotel in the neighborhood and get some sleep. How's that sound?"

"No," I said, scrunching the blanket into a knot. "You don't understand. I'm not leaving Tommy. I have to stay."

12

The light glared on overhead, yanking me out of a dream that seemed to tatter and drift away before I could catch hold of it. The sheet tangled around me as I struggled to sit up on the edge of the chair that had been flattened into a bed the night before.

"Need to get your temperature, young man, so's you can get ready to go home," said a big woman in a pink pantsuit as she headed toward Tommy and shoved a thermometer in his mouth. Tommy gagged. He made throwing-up noises.

"I don't think he knows what you're doing," I said, going over to the bed.

"Never had his temperature taken?" the woman said, pulling the thermometer away and then trying again, only this time under his arm.

"Not really, I don't think. Until last night."

"Is that a fact?" the woman said. "Guess you ought to know—you his sister? You sleep on that thing all right?"

I nodded. "Except I mostly didn't sleep. My father's around someplace, and a lot of the time he sat on that other chair and sometimes he'd go out in the hall and then come back and sit some more." I stopped for a minute and thought about how I had awakened during the night and seen him watching over Tommy and me, and how he had looked tense and ready to pounce—in case anyone tried to steal us away again.

"I've got to be moving on," the pink woman said, writing something on a chart. "But breakfast'll be along soon, and I'll see they bring enough for the two of you. You all take care now."

As soon as she was gone, I dug through one of the plastic bags, pulling out clean clothes, then headed into the bathroom to take a shower. Once I was dressed, I rolled my dirty clothes into a ball, and when I opened the door, I saw a nurse giving Tommy a dose of red medicine.

"Good morning," she said. "And before I forget— you were still sleeping when your dad left to get some breakfast. He didn't want to wake you so he said to tell you he'll be back soon. But if he'd waited a bit, I reckon you all three could have eaten off of this."

She pointed down at the tray on the high table next to the bed, and I saw that there were two of everything: milk and juice and cereal, scrambled eggs and toast and a whole stack of little packs of jelly. "Oh, wow," I said.

"The three of us and my grandmother and grandfather, too."

The nurse laughed and pushed a button that made the head of Tommy's bed go up. "Is he going to be able to manage this?" she said, looking at my brother, who was rocking his head and moaning.

"I'll help him," I said, unfolding one of the paper napkins and tucking it into the top of the green-and-yellow gown he was wearing. "Sometimes he eats better if you sort of pretend you don't care."

"Okay," the nurse said. "I'll leave you to it, but just push on that button if you need anything."

After she had gone, I pulled the tray table over the bed in front of Tommy. I peeled the plastic wrap off of the dishes and held a spoon up for him to see. When he didn't take it, I put it on one of the plates of eggs and piled toast next to it. "Eggs, Tommy," I said. "Good eggs and toast. And juice, too."

Standing beside the bed, I ate my half of everything. I watched out of the corner of my eye as my brother took one spoonful of eggs and then another and another. I was just licking the last bits of jelly off my fingers when I heard him say "Toast" in his flat-sounding voice. He rocked his head and said it again, this time sort of shouting it out. "Toast. Toast. Toast."

When he had done eating, Tommy rolled to one side and started fiddling with the plastic bracelet on his wrist, turning it faster and faster and staring down at it, the way he does when he sees anything that spins or twirls. "Hey, watch it, Tom-Tom. You're going to wear a hole in your arm doing that," I said. I put my hand out to stop him, and he shrugged me off, but not before I saw his name, Tommy McGee, printed on the bracelet.

"Tommy McGee," I whispered, thinking how the Tommy part was from now and the McGee part from our life before. "Tommy McGee—I guess that's who you are," I said as I slid the table away from the bed. Tommy kept on turning his bracelet while I sat on the edge of the chair-bed watching him and thinking about the night before and how I had told my father I knew who *I* was. Only now, this morning, I wasn't so sure. I mean, for four years my mother had called me *Elsie*—but now my father had come to get me, and I knew deep down that I couldn't be Elsie anymore. Same as I knew, after all this time, I couldn't go back to being L.C. I thought how last night Nana had kept saying *Linda*, but there didn't seem to be any *me* inside of Linda. And all of a sudden I knew I couldn't go on being any one of them. That all of those names had too much stuff attached to them, like dust balls sticking to a sweater on the closet floor.

Just then my father and grandmother and grand-father came into the room. "L.C., good morning," my father said.

Tears started running down my face, as if my eyes were a spigot I couldn't turn off. "That's just it," I said, rubbing at my eyes and getting up to meet them. "Don't you see? I've been thinking about what I said last night about how I knew who I was, only I didn't really. I can't be L.C. or Elsie either one, on account of all that's happened. And Linda doesn't *feel* like me." Then, without knowing where the words came from, I heard myself say, "From now on I want to be *Clay*. Because it's a starting-over kind of name."

"Clay?" said my father.

"Linda Clay?" said Nana.

I shook my head. "Just Clay."

Popoo nodded and pulled me close so that his sweater felt scratchy against my face. "My mother was Lily Clay," he said, "and my father sometimes called her just Clay, I think because he thought it was strong and feisty sounding, like she was. Like you are." He held me out at arm's length and looked at me. "Welcome, Clay."

A bunch of things happened before we were ready to leave the hospital. The doctor came in to check Tommy's throat and to leave a prescription. The whole time he was there, my brother, who by then was sitting straight up in bed, rocked back and forth and moaned a moan that turned into a howl. Dr. Greene and my father went out into the hall to talk and a little later called for me to join them so they could ask me questions. I told them about Tommy: about how he rocks and flaps his hands and hardly ever looks right at you; about how when he does talk, he sounds sort of like a robot and how he plays with his stones and puts them into rows. I told them how he seemed to live inside a glass bubble and not in the real world at all. Then they sent me back inside and talked some more.

Another thing that happened was that Sema James came to say good-bye. She stayed a really long time and walked along with us when the woman in the pink pantsuit pushed Tommy in a wheelchair down to the front door.

But the best thing of all happened when my dad went to get the car. The rest of us were waiting on the sidewalk in front of the hospital, watching the people going in and out, when Sema touched me on the arm and nodded off to one side. There was a woman standing there, pressed back against the wall. She was short and round and had on purple pants and a denim jacket and a funny, floppy camouflage hat. I caught my breath and stared for a minute before I grabbed Sema's hand, pulling her in that direction. "It's Vi," I said. "Come on."

Vi started toward us, and we met in the middle, next to a wooden tub with red flowers growing in it. "Well, Elsie McPhee, I see you're fixing to go home," she said.

"I'm Clay," I said. "From now on I'm Clay. Clay *McGee*." Then I stopped, with all the words I wanted to say bunched up somewhere inside of me.

"Mrs. Hassie and I talked last night," Sema said, "and I told her you'd be leaving today."

"And I reckoned I just had to come and say good-bye. Got my sister-in-law Emeline to mind the store, though she can't make a Shoot the Works the way I can, even if I do say so. That your brother over there? Is he some better?"

"Yes, a lot, but he still has to take medicine. You want to meet him, and my grandmother and grandfather, and my father, too?"

"I'd like that just fine," said Vi as we started over to where my father had just pulled into the curb and gotten out of the car. "I'm Violet Hassie," she said, holding her hand out to him. "A friend of Clay's."

"She owns the sub shop where I went yesterday when I ran out and—"

Then everybody started talking at once.

"We can't thank you enough . . ."

"How can we ever repay you . . ."

"So good to get involved . . ."

I stood on the sidewalk listening to them all talk and suddenly feeling cold and shivery, the way I had the day before when I had been alone with Tommy, waiting for help to come. Vi put her arm around my shoulders, and pulled me close. "We've gone on long enough, and now I'm going to let you folks get these children home, where they belong."

"Thank you," I managed to croak as she went on saying, "Good-bye, Tommy. Good-bye, Clay McGee. Have a good rest-of-your-life, the both of you."

I climbed in the middle of the backseat with my brother on one side and my grandfather on the other. Nana sat in front with my father.

"We all set?" asked Dad.

"All set," said Nana and Popoo at the same time.

"All set," I said. I stared out the window on the way through Richmond, determined to watch all the way to Baltimore, but soon a swooping tiredness came down around me, and I put my head back. I listened to Tommy's moan and the hum of the tires on the road and the faraway sound of the radio coming from the front seat. I closed my eyes.

13

I stood in the front hall of the house in
Baltimore and didn't know where I was. I mean, I
knew I was *home* because when we pulled into the
driveway, my father had said, "We're home now," and
Popoo said, "You're home, Clay," and Nana said, "It's
always good to get home." But in a spooky sort of way
I felt as though I'd wandered onto a movie set rather
than anyplace I'd ever been before. I looked at the
table, the lamp with the jangly things hanging off of
it, and the grandfather clock, then turned and walked
into the living room, stopping to stare at a picture on
the mantel of my mother, my father, baby Tommy,
and me. A long time ago.

I moved over to the piano where a music book was
open on the rack.

"The Skater's Waltz," said my father, coming up
behind me. "Remember how you used to play that?"

I looked at the page again, but the notes were

gibberish to me now. I saw the window seat at the end of the room and went toward it, reaching out to touch the flowered cushion at one end. "There was a cat named Tiger, and she always used to sleep here," I said. "Where is she?"

"I'm sorry, but Tiger died two years ago," my father said. "She was seventeen, so I guess in cat years she lived a good long life."

I sat down hard as dumb hot tears stung my eyes. I wanted to lash out at him, to say, *Why didn't you find me sooner so I could see Tiger? Why* didn't *you?* But I bit down hard on my bottom lip and swallowed back the words.

Dad sighed and sat beside me, and we stayed there like that, not saying anything till we heard a crash in the kitchen, followed by Tommy's voice shouting, "NO!" That's when we both got up and ran.

Nana, all splattered with milk, stood by the refrigerator. There were pieces of broken china on the floor as well as pickles and carrot sticks and half a sandwich. The other half-sandwich was clear across the room, but Tommy wasn't anywhere in sight.

"What happened?" Dad asked.

Nana sighed and blinked milk off her eyelashes. "Popoo went to the kennel to pick up the dog, and I gave Tommy his medicine, and that seemed to be okay. Then I asked him what he wanted for lunch, and when he didn't answer, I went ahead and made a peanut-butter-and-jelly sandwich, figuring all kids like that, but when I put it in front of him, he just—just sort of exploded." She shrugged and looked from Dad to me. "Did I do something wrong?"

"No, Mom, of course not, you did fine," my father said, but Nana still didn't look convinced.

"That's Tommy," I said, trying to explain. "That's the way he is sometimes. Especially when—I mean, he really really hates for things to change—and then yesterday— with the hospital and all—and now today, coming here—" I gave up and stooped to clean the mess off the floor.

"I'll take care of that," said Nana. "You and your father see to the boy. He headed that way, into the hall."

Dad and I went through the door, past the table with the jangly lamp, and almost fell over Tommy. He was sitting on the floor in front of the grandfather clock, staring at it and moving his head slowly from side to side with each swing of the pendulum.

"What're you doing, Tommy?" said Dad, getting down on the floor next to him.

"Are you hungry? It's way past lunchtime," I said, squatting on the other side. I leaned forward so that when he turned my way he was looking right at me, but his eyes were blank, and when the pendulum swung back, so did my brother's head.

Eventually I went into the kitchen and made another

peanut-butter-and-jelly sandwich. I wrapped it in a paper towel and went out into the hall, sitting next to Tommy and putting it on the floor in front of him. "Here's your lunch, Tom-Tom. Here's your favorite peanut butter and jelly."

"Is that what your mother did, feed him on the floor like a dog?" my father asked.

"Nuh-uh," I said, shaking my head. "That's not it at all, on account of Mom always said there was nothing *wrong* with Tommy, only I knew there was, and when he'd act up, she'd mostly leave it for me to deal with, and then I did—I had to do—whatever worked." Those same dumb hot tears stung my eyes again, and I looked away.

My father stood up. He touched me on the shoulder and held his hand out to me. "I didn't mean to criticize, Clay. I know you've been through a lot, and I'm going to be taking some time off from the office. We're going to get Tommy thoroughly evaluated to see just what his problems are and what can be done about them. Now, come along. Let's leave Tommy to his pendulum and go have some lunch. Okay?"

I followed my father back into the kitchen, trying to sort the hodgepodge of feelings that had settled around me. I mean, I was glad that someone was doing something about Tommy—but I was afraid of what we'd find out.

After lunch Dad said, "Why don't we go upstairs, and you can put your things away? Your old room is waiting for you." We went through the front hall where Tommy was still sitting on the floor, only this time Nana was there next to him. She had dumped his stones out of the Folgers can onto the rug, and as we passed by, he was beginning to sort them and line them up—the gray on one side and the white on the other.

I followed my father up the steps to the room at the end of the hall. "Here it is," he said. "Just the way you left it." And I stepped inside somebody else's world. It was the world of a somebody with about a million stuffed animals and Barbies and picture books and regular books and checkered ruffly curtains. The world of a somebody who was safe and secure and would never have to move in and out of places called Mountain Glen and Fair Meadows. Except it had all been fake—a lie—a—

"You see," my father said, "I didn't change a thing because I always knew I'd find you and your brother and bring you home." He dropped my plastic bags of clothes onto the bed and added, "I'm going to leave you to look around a bit while I make a couple of phone calls, but I'll be right down the hall, in my room. Okay?"

I said okay and waited till Dad was all the way back to his own room before I took a handful of clothes out of one of the bags and carried them over to the dresser. I pulled open the top drawer and stood staring down at neat little stacks of underwear and socks and tights and hair holders, feeling sort of as if I'd moved into someplace, only the other tenant hadn't quite moved out yet. I dropped my own stuff on the floor and opened the second drawer, and the third, picking up these really small T-shirts and shorts and sweaters that I realized used to belong to me but that I didn't remember. After a couple of minutes I scrunched all my *then* clothes into the bottom drawer and arranged my *now* ones in the others.

When I was done with that, I stood staring at the things on the top of the dresser, running my fingers over a pink comb-and-brush set and an empty bottle of Little Miss toilet water. I picked up a conch shell, holding it to my ear and listening to the ocean roar. I opened the top of a white plastic jewelry box, and a ballerina started to dance, spinning on her toes to a tinkling kind of music. I watched her twirl, and all of a sudden it was Christmas morning and I was sitting next to the tree, unwrapping the box and opening it, watching this same ballerina dance. The music stopped, and I was back in the present again as I wound the key on the bottom of the box and set her to dancing again.

From there I wandered over to the bookcase, searching the shelves till I found my Ramona books on the bottom shelf. I found *The Cat in the Hat* and flipped it open, reading the words out loud just as slowly and carefully as I remembered doing when I first discovered I *could* read them. Still holding tight to the book, I rooted through a boxful of Barbies and then moved on to examine my old Kirsten doll sitting in her own little chair under the window with her wardrobe full of clothes beside her. I sifted through her outfits, taking her white fleecy nightgown and holding it against my face as I thought about how I used to dress Kirsten in it every night when it was time for the two of us to go to bed.

I moved on to the closet, opening the door and looking at the too-small dresses and skirts and an old winter coat. Suddenly I remembered all the things we had left behind in Richmond: our other jeans, our jackets and slickers, my summer sandals, and Tommy's cowboy boots. Would we ever see them again, and would our father know we didn't have them, and if he did, would he get us new stuff, and what would we wear if he didn't? And what if he decided it was too much trouble having us back again and started getting sorry he'd come after us? What then?

I was still standing there thinking when I heard a thumpety-thumpety sound on the steps and out in the hall, and Sandy burst into the room, sniffing me and pushing at the backs of my knees so that I sat down in a heap and wrapped my arms around him. "Oh, Sandy," I said, pressing my face into his side, breathing in his sharp doggy smell, "I remember everything about you." I ran my hands over his big head and along the feathers of hair on the backs of his legs.

Just then Popoo appeared in the doorway. "Oh, good, he found you," he said. "That's one smart dog—I said 'Go find L.C.,' and he took right off. Up the stairs to where you were." He held his hand out. "Now I know, it's Clay, but we have to give Sandy time to adjust. You know what they say about old dogs and new tricks. Maybe that goes for names, too. Anyhow, why don't we go out front and play some ball with him? I never think dogs get enough exercise in the kennel."

We played ball on the front lawn, with Popoo throwing the ball once to me and then to Sandy, once to Nana, to Dad, to Tommy, and always to Sandy in between. When anyone threw the ball to Tommy, though, he'd always just let it roll down his body, same as he let Sandy's slobbery kisses roll off his face. I mean, he just stood there like a tree or a fence post or something.

We played ball like that for an absolute age, mostly I guess because nobody could figure out what we'd do if we stopped. After a while Tommy sat down on the grass and Nana settled onto the front porch, leaning back against a post, but Dad and Popoo and Sandy and I kept going. Back and forth and down toward the hedge for Sandy. Back and forth and—

"Look, Clay," my father said, taking the ball from the dog and wiping the spit on the back of his khakis, "there're a couple of friends here to see you." He nodded in the direction of the bushes between our house and the one next door, calling, "Come on over, girls. Look who's here."

I turned in time to see two girls pushing their way through the bushes. One had black curly hair, and the other was blond, with a ponytail. They both had on shorts, though it wasn't all that warm, and baggy yellow T-shirts with SOCCER IS ALL in red letters across the front. I stood staring at them, same as they were staring at me, with none of us saying anything. Finally the dark-haired girl took a step forward, and then another, motioning for her friend to follow. They stopped and stared some more until the blonde finally said, "L.C.? Is that really you? My mom saw your grandfather, and he said you were back and—"

"I'm back, but I'm not L.C. on account of I'm Clay now," I said, watching as they came a step closer.

"Clay? That's pretty cool. You know who we are?"

A lot of old stuff came crowding back, swirling around me. "Margaret," I said, changing it from a question to a statement before the word was all the way out of my mouth. "Margaret from next door." I turned to the dark-haired girl and said, "And Lily from across the street."

"See," said Margaret, fake-punching Lily on the arm, "I told you she'd remember." Then they took giant steps the rest of the way to where I was standing beside my father. We maybe would have stood that way forever, not knowing what to say next, if Nana hadn't said, "Why don't you girls come inside, and I'll make some lemonade. I'm sure you have a lot of catching up to do."

"Thanks anyway, Mrs. McGee," said Margaret, "but yesterday was my birthday, and we still have cake left and my mom said to bring L.C.—I mean Clay—back there for some. Besides, I've got a new Boomerangs CD, and Lily and I were going to listen to it. Don't you just think they're the greatest, Clay?"

I took a step back, closer to my father, wondering who the Boomerangs were and what I was supposed to know about them.

"Why don't you go, Clay? It would be fun," said Dad, putting his hand between my shoulder blades, I guess to keep me from going any farther back and disappearing into the house. "Tommy'll be fine here with us. I want him to rest anyway."

While I was still trying to decide whether to go, Margaret and Lily went over to where Tommy was sitting, dropping down on the ground next to him. "Hi, Timmy. D'you remember me? I'm Margaret, and I used to pull you in your wagon," Margaret said.

"He's Tommy now, and he's got to stay Tommy," I

said, moving close to them. Then Tommy began to rock and yank the grass out in tufts till there was a round bare spot in front of him.

"Is he shy?" asked Lily.

"Yeah, I guess," I said. "Something like that. And there're things he doesn't understand."

"You run along, Clay. Go with the girls," said Dad as he came across the lawn. And next thing I knew, I was pushing my way between the bushes, following after Margaret and Lily.

The inside of Margaret's house smelled the way I suddenly remembered it smelling—sort of warm and spicy sweet. As we were heading to the kitchen, a little girl in red overalls came barreling through the door, butting her head against Margaret's legs and looking up at me and saying, "Who are you?"

"I'm Clay, who are you?"

"I'm Polly," the child said as she started to giggle.

"Yeah," said Margaret. "That's Polly the pest, and she's my sister."

"But you don't *have* a sister," I said.

"I do now. She's three years old."

I took hold of a chair to steady myself, sort of feeling as though I was trying to catch a feather blowing just out of reach. Then Margaret's mother, Mrs. Shaska, was there, holding me at arm's length to look at me and pulling me close for a hug. We went on into the kitchen and ate cake and drank lemonade, and all the while I could tell Mrs. Shaska was dying to ask me questions about where I'd been and how my father found me and where my mother was. She didn't, though, and mostly I just sat there and listened to the rest of them talk about people I didn't know and movies I hadn't seen and bands I'd never heard.

"You know something, Clay," said Lily, "there're a bunch of fifth grades at our school, and Margaret and I aren't together, but maybe you'll end up with one of us."

"If they give you a choice, pick mine," said Margaret. "Only they'll probably just *tell* you because that's the way schools are."

"Well, yeah, I guess," I said as I felt my insides turn to Jell-O and my knees start to shake. I mean, for all those years I'd bugged my mom to let me go to school, and now—I didn't want to go.

After we put our dishes in the dishwasher, we went upstairs to Margaret's room, which wasn't where it used to be. "This isn't your room," I said, stopping in the doorway.

"It is now," Margaret said. "When Polly was born, my mother and father moved me in here and gave the baby my old room because it was closer to theirs. Anyway, this is bigger. You like it?"

"Yeah, it's great," I said, going the rest of the way in and looking around at the posters on the walls, the plaid bedspreads, the heap of cushions on the floor. I sat on a chair by the door and watched as Margaret took a CD out of its case and put it on to play.

"These guys are awesome, just listen," she said as she and Lily stretched out, one on each of the beds.

The music was loud and the beat pulsed inside my head, but I couldn't concentrate, and when the CD was only partway done, I got up and tiptoed out of the room and down the stairs. I eased my way out the front door and pushed my way back through the bushes. I went across the lawn to my father's house, thinking about Manda back in Delaware and how, right at that moment, I felt as though I knew her better than I did these two old best friends.

14

That night I slept on the floor next to my brother's bed. I started out in my own room—my *old* room, from before—and waited until Nana and Popoo had gone home and Dad was asleep before I tiptoed down the hall by the glow of the nightlight. Somehow it made me feel better having Tommy close by, even if it meant listening to his snuffly, snorty breathing.

I slept there the next night, too, and the next and the next, getting up early each morning and sneaking back to my bed in the Barbie room. I mean, I didn't want my father to find me and think I wasn't glad to be home, because I was. It's just that glad didn't exactly feel the way I thought it would.

The weird thing was that after I had been doing that for a string of nights, I woke up one morning with a red-and-white blanket wrapped around me and sort of tucked under my head. I dragged that blanket behind me when I went back to my room, shoving it onto the shelf in my closet. But when I went down to breakfast, neither my dad nor I said anything—except hi and regular morning things like that. What was *really* weird, though, was that that night I went to sleep in my own bed and stayed there till morning, tangled (and sweaty) in the red-and-white blanket.

While all this night stuff was happening, a lot was going on during the days, too. Some good, some not so good.

Topping the not-so-good list was our trip to the dentist, mostly because Tommy sat on the floor in front of the fish tank and watched the gold and silver and purple fish flicker through the water and wouldn't move. He wouldn't move when Dad and I tried to coax him up, or when the dental hygienist sat down beside him and tried to show him a giant toothbrush. He wouldn't move when Dr. Milhaus himself came out to get him. In fact, that's when Tommy stared even harder at the fish, moaning and rocking until the dentist rubbed his hands together and said, "Maybe this isn't a very good time to check on Tommy's teeth."

The next day my father took us to the pediatrician because, except for Tommy's recent trip to the hospital, neither one of us had seen a doctor the whole time we were away. We didn't say it out loud, but I was pretty sure Dad was as worried as I was about how Tommy would act and what we'd do if he planted himself on the floor again and refused to budge. Once we got there, though, I forgot about my brother and father and everything else because the minute we stepped into the waiting room, I was back to being a little kid again. I remembered it all: the long, skinny windows that went almost to the floor; the regular-size furniture and the little chairs and tables, too; the shelves of books and puzzles alongside the basket of toy cars; the giant pictures of poison oak and poison ivy on the wall behind the desk. When the secretary called my name, my father asked me if I wanted to go in to see the doctor by myself and I said yes and started down the hall to the office, without even waiting for the nurse to show me the way.

Dr. Callum, when she stood up to greet me, looked just the way I remembered her: tall and thin and sort of stooped (I guess from leaning over to talk to children so much), with her hair pulled back in a sagging ponytail. She took hold of both my hands, smiling at me and saying, "It's good to see you, L.C., and I know kids hate to hear this, but I really have to say it—my how you've grown."

"Clay," I said, still holding on to her hands. "It's Clay now—*I'm* Clay now, I mean."

"Okay, then, it's good to see you, Clay," Dr. Callum said as she steered me to the chair next to her desk, the one where my mother used to sit and hold me on her lap when I was little. First she asked me questions about colds and allergies and upset stomachs, and if I'd had them. Then she had me get up on the table in the examining room and tapped and thumped me all over, looking in my eyes and ears and down my throat.

"Well, Clay, I'd say you're a picture of health," Dr. Callum said as she helped me down and led the way back to her office. "I'll see you next year, unless something comes up, and in the meantime"—she stopped for a minute as if she was not quite sure she should say what she was going to say—"Well, yes, I'm going to give your father the name of someone you might want to talk to. Sometimes when a person's been through what you've been through, it helps to talk about it. Don't you think?"

I don't know because nobody ever does—not my father or my grandmother or my grandfather, not Lily or Margaret, either, I thought. *Everybody's being super nice, but nobody ever asks me what it was like when we were away or what I thought about or what I did.* I didn't say any of this but just mumbled "I guess" as I stared at the picture of Dr. Callum's two children on the wall over her desk. "That's Kerry and Anna," she said and pressed a button on her phone and asked the secretary to send my father and Tommy in. "Why don't you stay while I examine your brother?" she said, turning to me. "He'll probably be more relaxed that way."

I'm not sure that Tommy was relaxed, but he didn't moan and he didn't rock and he let Dr. Callum check him all over. When she asked him questions, he didn't answer them and instead of looking at her he watched the ceiling fan as it swooshed around and around.

When she had finished examining him, Dr. Callum asked me to take Tommy back to the waiting room so she and Dad could talk. As soon as we got there, I settled him onto one of the little chairs and piled a mess of toy cars on the table in front of him, rolling them back and forth and making engine noises in my throat. Tommy flapped his hands. He stared over my head, not seeing me or the cars or the set of twins having a tug-of-war with an orange blanket right next to him. The mother of the twins kept looking at him in that way that grownups have when they're gawking at something but pretending they're not, and for a minute I wanted to flap my own hands at her and stare and maybe moan a little, to see what she would do. I didn't though.

Dad finally came to get us, saying, "Okay, kids. Let's be on our way. It's almost lunchtime." He helped me put the toys in the basket and steered Tommy out to the car, fastening his seat belt around him. We were just pulling off the parking lot when my father said, "Well, Clay, Dr. Callum thinks you're both the picture of health."

"What'd she say?" I asked.

"That you're both the picture of health."

"No. What'd she *really* say? About Tommy. You

stayed back there to talk, so she must've said some-thing."

"Well, yes, she's going to set up some appointments at Hopkins to have him thoroughly evaluated. We'll know more after that."

"Yes, but what did she *say*?" I suddenly felt as if everything in my head was going to explode. "She's a doctor and doctors know these things, so what did she say? I need to know that."

My father sighed and glanced in his rearview mirror to check on Tommy. "Dr. Callum said she thinks—same as I've thought all along and same as Dr. Greene in Richmond suspected—that Tommy is autistic."

"Artistic?" I said. "How can he be? I mean, he can't even draw, and when he does, he scribble-scrabbles."

"*Au*tistic," my father said. "It's not the same thing. Not the same thing at all."

"What *is* it then?"

Dad pulled over to the curb and stopped the car. He sighed and turned to face me. "Autism is a little hard to explain, and I'm not sure I really understand it myself," he said.

"Is it like mumps or measles or tonsilitis?" I said. "What are they going to do about it?"

My father shook his head. "I'm afraid it's not that simple. The way I understand it is that autism is a syndrome rather than a disease, which means it's a series of symptoms that all point to a certain condition. For example, that would include the way Tommy rocks and flaps his hands, the way he moans and won't look anyone in the eye and puts his stones in rows, over and over again."

"But they'll fix it, right? The doctors, I mean. They'll do something to make him the way he's meant to be, won't they?" I said, watching my father as he watched me.

"As I said, it's not that easy." Dad stopped, and I could almost see him giving himself a push to get started again. "Very often—in a large percentage of cases—children with autism are mentally retarded, too."

I turned to look at my brother, thinking about how he couldn't read or make his letters or even count, how he couldn't draw a stick man or point to who was the mouse and who was the boy in his favorite book. I reached out to touch him, but he pulled away, staring at the dome light and starting to rock.

When my father spoke again, his voice was softer than it had been before and sort of choky. "Maybe this *is* the way Tommy's meant to be—and if it is, you know, we'll love him the same as we always have." Dad shook his head and cleared his throat and turned the key to start the car. "Anyway, I didn't mean to sound like the voice of doom here. There's a lot of help out there, so let's wait to see what the doctors at Hopkins have to say, and what they suggest. And whatever the diagnosis, Tommy's going to need a great deal of intensive work, maybe even a special school. But we can handle that, can't we, Clay?"

I nodded, and Dad reached out to squeeze my hand as he pulled into traffic.

Dr. Callum called that afternoon to tell my father that Tommy's appointments at Hopkins were scheduled for the following week. The time in between, while we were waiting, both dragged and raced along, like a clock that was sometimes slow and sometimes fast, ringing out the hours one right after the other.

We went to the aquarium one day, and Nana and Popoo and I had a great time looking at the fish and watching the dolphin show, but my father and brother never made it out of the lobby. That's on account of right when you go in the front door, there are these columns with blue water inside (unless they're blue columns with regular water—I'm not sure which) that just keep bubbling all the time. Tommy took one look at them and sat down, sort of in the middle, and stared at the bubbles till it was time to leave.

Another day Nana and I went shopping. First we went to a department store and looked at the kind of clothes my grandmother thought kids my age should wear. I put them on, turning this way and that in front of the mirror as I tried to figure out how to explain that these didn't look anything like the clothes Lily and Margaret wore.

"Try the smaller stores in the mall," the saleswoman whispered as Nana paid her for the socks and underwear and pajamas. "That's where I take my daughter."

We went to the Gap and Limited Too, and Nana let me try on a ton of stuff. We finally settled on new jeans and a couple of pairs of shorts and shirts and even a tank top that I could tell she didn't like—because of the way her nose twitched when she saw me in it. "You'll have to keep me current, Clay," Nana said as we were eating pizza in the food court. "I don't want your friends to think your grandmother is a fossil."

On Saturday Mrs. Shaska took Margaret and Lily and me to the movies, which was the first time that I'd really gone anywhere without my father or one of my grandparents. I wanted to see it, and it was okay—sort of soppy but okay—but once I got there and was sitting in the theater in the dark, the whole time I was trying to watch the screen, I had to keep telling myself that nobody was going to steal me away again. Finally I gave up trying to follow the story and concentrated instead on holding tight to the armrests and looking over my shoulder from time to time and planning how I'd lock my feet under the seat in front if anyone tried to get me.

When the show was over and Margaret's mother asked if we'd like to stop for ice cream, I said "no" straight out, before anybody else could answer. Mrs. Shaska looked at me and felt my head and said I looked a little peaked and maybe I was coming down with something and that we'd stop for ice cream another time.

The day my father took Tommy to see the doctors, Popoo and I went to the SPCA. When Dad told me he and Tommy, just the two of them, were going to Hopkins, I didn't know what to think. I mean, I *always* went with Tommy. *Everywhere.* Besides, he *needed* me. It was my *job*.

"It's going to be a long day, Clay. Lots of waiting in one office after another," said Dad, setting his jaw in a way I knew from long ago meant: This is how it's going to be.

"Besides," said Popoo, "you promised to help me pick out a puppy, remember? And today's the day."

It could've been yesterday, I thought. Or tomorrow, or maybe next week. I was still trying to decide whether to say that out loud when my father put his arm around my shoulder and pulled me close. "You know, Clay," he said, "through the years you've taken amazing and wonderful care of your brother—better care than anyone had a right to expect from someone your age—and we're all very proud of you. But now—and I know this is going to be hard—now it's time to let others take over some. Tommy's going to have to get used to a lot of people—a neurologist, a psychologist, a child psychiatrist, a speech therapist, to name just a few. And today seems to me to be a good day to start. So while Tommy and I are off at Hopkins, what I'd like you to do is go with Popoo and pick out the most special dog in the place. Deal?"

My face was against my father's chest, and when I nodded, his shirt rubbed against my cheek and I could hear his heart beat. "Deal," I said.

Popoo and I knew right from the start that Daisy was the most special dog at the SPCA. And there were lots of dogs to choose from—big ones and little ones, grownup dogs and puppies. Daisy was yellow with big floppy feet, which my grandfather said meant she was going to be a big floppy dog. She had chocolate eyes, and the hair on the inside of her ears was soft and fuzzy, and when the attendant took her out of the cage, she tugged at my shoelaces as if to say, "Come on, let's get out of here."

And we did. Get out of there, after Popoo signed the papers and the woman in the office gave us a list of the shots that Daisy had already had and the ones she still needed to have. On the way home we stopped at PetsMart and I put Daisy in the cart and pushed her through the store while Popoo selected a leash and collar and a bag of Puppy Chow and two metal bowls. From there we went back to my grandparents' house and introduced Daisy to Nana and Sandy.

"That's a great puppy," said Nana, bending over to pat her. Sandy wasn't so sure. He sniffed Daisy all over and stood still for a minute while she tugged on his ears and nipped at his heels, then he shook her off and went to take a nap under a forsythia bush.

When my father and brother were done at the hospital, they came back to Nana and Popoo's for dinner. "It was a hard day, right, son?" Dad said as he pushed Tommy's chair into the table. I can't exactly figure if my father thinks that someday Tommy's going to answer him like a regular boy, but this time the way he answered was to shove his plate of lasagna onto the floor, to spill his milk, to howl.

We made it through dinner somehow and afterward went out to the patio where the grownups had coffee, and Dad told us about the day at Hopkins and how, even though they had to go back next week, the opinion was that Tommy was autistic. The whole time that he was talking, Daisy was rolling and tumbling and chasing shadows to make us laugh, even though we were feeling incredibly sad.

"You know something, Clay," Popoo said as we were

getting ready to leave, "I don't think Sandy's going to take kindly to this young pup, so the way I see it, you'd be doing me a favor by taking Daisy home to live at your house. How about it? Can you do that?"

I looked at my grandfather and I looked at my father, and I was pretty sure they had cooked this up between them. I looked at Nana and she winked at me and I winked back. "I can do that," I said. "I can definitely do that."

Later that night, after Tommy was in bed, Dad and I sat in the family room watching Daisy sleep. We talked some more about Tommy and what the doctors had said. We talked about training Daisy and how I was going to have to teach her to walk on a leash and to sit and stay and come when I told her to. We talked about the therapist Dr. Callum wanted me to see and about how Popoo, because he was a retired teacher, was going to tutor me now and on through the summer. We talked about maybe going to the beach and—just everything.

Except my mother.

15

Nobody talked about my mother. My father didn't, Nana and Popoo didn't, and Lily and Margaret didn't, either. That was one of the things I brought up when I went to see Rose, the therapist Dr. Callum sent me to. I told her a bunch of other stuff, too—about New Jersey and Delaware and Richmond. We even discussed Manda and how, though I never knew her all that well, I sometimes wrote letters to her in my head, telling her what had happened.

"You could write them out. Maybe even mail them," Rose said. I thought about that, but as time went on, I didn't much feel I had to do it. Besides, it was the part about my mother that really bothered me.

"Why *doesn't* anyone ever talk about her? My mother, I mean," I said one day when Rose and I were sitting in the fat and squishy chairs in her office. "Why don't they?"

"Why don't you? Talk about *her* to *them*," she

answered. But the weird thing was, I never could.

Until that Saturday in June.

We were hanging out in the Shaskas' backyard trying to think of something to do when Lily said, "Hey, that was cool, seeing your mom's picture in the paper today, Clay."

"My mom?" I said, hoping my voice didn't sound as croaky on the outside as it felt on the inside.

"On the front page of the Maryland section. You saw it, didn't you?"

"Yeah, sure. I didn't know you meant that picture," I said.

Margaret gave Lily a jab with her elbow, and right away started talking about how there was nothing else to do so why didn't we go inside and make brownies. When we went in, though, Mrs. Shaska said "maybe later" to the brownies because she had to leave in a few minutes to take Margaret to get new tennis shoes. After that I hung around just long enough to look casual before I took off through the bushes to my own yard.

Once inside I found the paper on the kitchen table, but the Maryland section was missing. I upended the recycling bag on the floor and sorted through last week's papers but it wasn't there, either. I raced through the dining room and living room and sunporch, checking tabletops, flipping sofa cushions, and peering behind chairs. Daisy woke up from her nap and chased after me as I ran upstairs, checking my own room in case Dad had put it there for me to see. I searched my father's bedroom, shifting piles of magazines on the night table and even checking in the clothes hamper in the bathroom.

I found Dad working with Tommy at a table in my brother's room. "Where is it?" I said, standing in front of him. "I've hunted through this whole house, and I have to know—so where is it?"

"Where is what?" my father asked.

"I already know, so don't pretend. Lily told me. She said it was cool seeing my mother's picture in the paper today, and I didn't know what she was talking about and then I had to lie and pretend I did, and then when I came home and tried to find it I couldn't. So where is it?"

Dad got up and went to his room. I heard the closet door open and close, and in a minute he was back, handing me the paper. When I unfolded it, my mother was staring up at me, her cloud of dark hair hanging long and lank and not at all the way it used to be. "I'm sorry, Clay. I don't know, I guess I was just trying to spare you," my father said.

And for a minute, after I had ahold of the paper, I wasn't sure what to do with it. "Should I read it?" I asked.

"I think you'd better," Dad said. "And then, if you have any questions—"

I read the article slowly, first standing where I was and then sitting on the edge of Tommy's bed. It told a lot of stuff I already knew, about how my mother had abducted Tommy and me and how we'd moved from place to place until our father found us and brought us back. Then it went on to say that after a hearing she'd been freed on bail and how, after that, the judge had said he wouldn't make her go to jail if she would agree to long-term psychiatric treatment.

"Where is she now?" I asked. "Where is my mother now?"

"Living with her sister, your aunt Joan, in Columbia. And from what I understand she's seeing a doctor, working hard at understanding why, instead of being able to stay and face whatever the problem was with Tommy, she felt she had to take the two of you and run away. Why she had to keep on running, all those years. She has a long way to go, but your mom has made a start. What else can I tell you?"

"When can I see her?" I said. "You can tell me that."

It's July now, and I've been to see my mother once. We met in an office downtown, and my father drove me there and waited outside. There was someone else there, too—a woman from Child Protective Services—who will be there for every visit and stay the whole time on account of that's the way the judge said it had to be. Her name was Sharon, and before I went I wondered if she'd be anything like Sema James in Richmond, but she wasn't.

I worried a lot about what it would be like, between my mom and me. I mean, would she still be totally mad at me for doing what I did in Richmond, for getting the FBI to come and all? Would *I* still be mad at *her* for taking us away, for stealing those years from Tommy and me? When I asked Rose those questions ahead of time, she smiled and said, "Just relax, Clay, and be your natural self, and it'll be okay."

And it was okay. Sort of. Especially after we got past that scary beginning part of not knowing what to say. Though to tell the truth, we never got really chatty. Not once during the whole visit.

The first thing I noticed when I went in was that my mother looked somehow tamer and less wild-eyed. Her hair had been cut and seemed to fit her head like a cap. She had on khakis and a navy blue shirt, which wasn't all that different from what she usually wore, except that in a weird kind of way they seemed *quieter*.

"You've grown, Elsie," she said, reaching out and then pulling her hand back.

"Clay."

"Yes, I heard about the name. You've grown, Clay."

"Yeah, I guess," I said and then couldn't think of what should come next.

"And your brother? How's Tommy?"

"He's good." And because the last thing in the world I wanted to do was get in a conversation about Tommy, I said, "I went to the movies with Margaret and Lily, and Mrs. Shaska went, too. But what I really liked was the aquarium."

"I remember taking you there when you were little," my mother said. "Do they still have the dolphin show?"

I told her yes, and then we were stuck. The silence seemed to bang and clatter around us till finally Sharon moved her chair closer and said, "I love the aquarium, especially the sharks. What did you like best, Clay?"

"The dolphins, I guess. And the puffins. And lunch, of course. I always like lunch." Sharon and my mother laughed, and then we were stuck again.

"Your hair looks cool," I said to Mom after what seemed like hours.

"Yeah, it is, in this hot weather," she said.

"No, I mean cool as in *cool*. You know."

"Oh—thank you," she said.

And because I was afraid we were going to slip back into one of those bottomless pits of silence, I said, "I might get mine cut, too. I mean, I've been thinking about it, and Nana said she'd take me."

"That would look nice, I think," said Mom. "I just wish I could take you."

And without thinking or meaning to, either one, I

pulled back in my chair.

"To get your hair cut, I mean," my mother said. "I wish I could take you there."

"Oh, yeah."

"But maybe someday."

After that we talked a little bit about Aunt Joan in Columbia and about the weather and about Daisy and all the things I was going to teach her to do. Then it was time for the visit to be over. Sharon went to stand by the door. My mother and I stood up.

"I just want you to know that you did what you had to do," she said. "That you did the right thing. I wish it could've been better—between us, I mean—but I'm working at it and learning, and it will be someday. I promise."

I moved toward her and we gave each other an awkward kind of hug, and the funny thing was, my mother smelled just the way I remember her smelling from when I was a little girl. Like cinnamon and oranges and maybe the ocean, all at the same time.

Afterward my dad took me home and we ordered Chinese carryout. Once supper was done, Dad and Tommy and Daisy and I sat out back and watched the fireflies, and I thought about the ton of stuff that was going on in my life.

About how I'll get to see my mother every week from now on, and how maybe eventually Tommy will be able to go with me, too. I thought about the trip to the beach with Nana and Popoo in August and about my sessions with Rose and how I'm just beginning to tell her that sometimes I'm still afraid of someone stealing me away again. When I'm being sensible I know it isn't going to happen, but it helps to talk. I thought about Tommy, too, and how it may be my imagination, but he doesn't seem to rock as much as he did before, and how, when I talk to him, sometimes I could swear he looks straight at me. At least for a while.

And I thought about Popoo, and what a good teacher he is, and how hard he makes me work. But that's okay, because when sixth grade starts in the fall, I, Clay McGee, am going to be there.